# "Someone is tailgating us," Ryan said.

Nadia twisted so she could see the car behind hers and Ryan's. The SUV rammed the back of their vehicle. Nadia jerked forward as the car slid, fishtailing, but Ryan kept them on the road. He guided them out of the skid and revved the engine, sending them flying forward.

The SUV sped up, hitting them again and sending Nadia crashing into the dashboard.

"Nadia! Are you okay?"

She groaned. Ryan risked a glance at her. Blood trickled from a gash on her forehead.

The SUV hit them again, sending them into a tailspin. Ryan fought to regain control of the car as the tires slipped off the road and the car headed down an embankment.

"Ryan!" Nadia screamed.

Brush flew by as he pumped the brakes, trying to slow the car. Several large oaks at the foot of the embankment loomed. Ryan wrenched the wheel to the right moments before the sound of crumpling metal filled the air...

# PURSUIT OF THE TRUTH

———

## K.D. RICHARDS

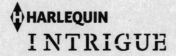

To Delria, who taught me I could do anything,
and to Neil, who makes anything possible.

Recycling programs
for this product may
not exist in your area.

ISBN-13: 978-1-335-40153-3

Pursuit of the Truth

Copyright © 2021 by Kia Dennis

This edition published by arrangement with Harlequin Books S.A.

For questions and comments about the quality of this book,
please contact us at CustomerService@Harlequin.com.

Harlequin Enterprises ULC
22 Adelaide St. West, 40th Floor
Toronto, Ontario M5H 4E3, Canada
www.Harlequin.com

**Printed in U.S.A.**

**K.D. Richards** is a native of the Washington, DC, area, who now lives outside Toronto with her husband and two sons. You can find her at kdrichardsbooks.com.

### Books by K.D. Richards

### Harlequin Intrigue

*Pursuit of the Truth*

Visit the Author Profile page at Harlequin.com.

## CAST OF CHARACTERS

*Nadia Shelton*—The CEO of Shelton Hotels is determined to find out the truth about her brother's apparent death.

*Ryan West*—The co-owner of West Securities has carried a secret torch for Nadia for over a year and will not allow anyone to hurt her.

*Nathan Shelton*—The former CEO of Shelton Hotels and Nadia's brother faked his own death in an effort to avoid the consequences of a deadly mistake.

*Shawn West*—Co-owner of West Securities always has his brother's back.

*Olivia Bennett*—Nadia's administrative assistant and best friend.

*Erik Jackson*—Nadia and Nathan's uncle and Shelton Hotel's accountant has secrets of his own to protect.

*Mike Dexter*—The president of rival hotel corporation Aurora Hotels and Nadia's former boyfriend is determined to purchase Shelton Hotels, whether Nadia wants to sell or not.

# Chapter One

Goose bumps tingled over Nadia Shelton's arms and neck as she exited her apartment building. She scanned the morning commuters looking for signs of someone watching her. And like every previous morning, all she saw were fellow New Yorkers hustling along the sidewalk, somewhat faster this morning than the morning before, as the gray clouds overhead pelted them with rain.

Nadia pulled her purse and briefcase closer to her body, hoping to shield them from the worst of the rain, and tightened her grip on her umbrella. The hairs on the back of her neck stood at attention as she entered the flow of bodies on the sidewalk. There was no time for paranoia. She was already ten minutes late getting to work. Granted, that was not typically a huge deal since she was her own boss, but this morning she had a meeting she did not want to be late for.

*Should have thought of that while you were primping for a certain security specialist with sexy hazel eyes.*

Nadia caught a glimpse of herself in the large

front window of the corner bodega. She slowed and examined her reflection as she passed by. Her plum-colored sheath accentuated the curve of her hips and popped vibrantly against her dark skin. The dress showed just a hint of her ample cleavage—sexy, but still work-appropriate. The off-white trench coat she'd slid into on her way out the door completed the look. She'd dressed to feel good about herself, and looking into the storefront window, she felt as if she'd succeeded.

Goodness knows she deserved some happiness. The last several months had been the most trying of her life.

She took a step away from the window, then jerked to a stop once again when the reflection of a man on the other side of the street caught her eye. He huddled under the awning of a bookstore, its interior lights still darkened.

Nadia strained to make out his features, but the window distorted his image, even as scores of people hurried by, making it even more difficult to get a clear view. She mentally noted the dark hoodie, navy jeans and black work boots before starting down the sidewalk again, her heart rate picking up its pace.

She shot a glance over her shoulder, but the man had moved from the doorway.

*You're being paranoid.* He was probably just taking a reprieve from the rain.

There was absolutely no reason for anyone to be watching her, and any other day, she probably wouldn't have even noticed the man. But this hadn't been the only odd occurrence lately. An image jumped into her head. Born and raised in New York, she'd seen her fair share of rats, even dead ones, but never mangled so horribly.

She shook her head to clear the memory of the rat from her mind. Her neighbor's cat had most likely left that little gift for her—it couldn't be anything more sinister than that.

And her keyed car and the late-night hang-ups? Was the cat behind those things too?

*Stop.*

It wasn't as if the garage she parked her rarely used car in was Fort Knox. Teenagers had probably keyed the car. And the hang-ups could be teenagers too. Or telemarketers. Or simply a wrong number. Repeated every night for the last two weeks?

She chewed her bottom lip as she hurried along the sidewalk, dodging open umbrellas. She was overreacting. The pressures of being thrust into the role of CEO of Shelton Hotels was making her jumpy. And anxious. And short-tempered.

Nadia drew in a breath and exhaled slowly, her therapist's advice not to be so hard on herself echoing in her mind. The last year had brought a lot of change, and it would take time to settle into a new normal.

For six years, she and her older brother, Nathan, had run Shelton Hotels, the company their father built from nothing into a small chain of boutique hotels in New York City. As vice president of operations, Nadia concentrated on the day-to-day workings of the three hotels they owned, specifically their flagship hotel in Harlem where she kept her primary office. CEO Nate handled the big-picture stuff and was the face of the company.

That had all changed when Nate died in a car accident eleven months ago.

Nadia had inherited Shelton Hotels, lock, stock, and barrel. As the newly minted CEO, it was up to her alone to keep the family legacy intact. Not everybody believed she could pull it off.

She reached the corner a block from the hotel as the stoplight changed from green to yellow and the pedestrian walk signal flashed a warning against crossing.

"Excuse me," a voice boomed in her ear, making her jump and gasp.

A tall man skirted around her, long coat flapping around his thighs, his briefcase held atop his head as a shield against the rain. Nadia frowned as the man dashed across the street without a backward glance.

Her frown deepened when her gaze fell on the bus shelter beside her. An advertisement for Aurora Hotels and Suites hung on the wall of the shelter. Aurora wasn't direct competition since it was consistently ranked in the luxury-hotel market, rather than the midscale market like Shelton. But she'd dated the president of Aurora briefly, and the whole affair had soured her on the man and the company he ran.

She tore her eyes from the offending advertisement and, following the lead of all the other commuters waiting for the light to change, pulled her phone from her coat pocket. She'd barely swiped the screen awake when big hands landed on her shoulder blades. She twisted to see who was behind her, but a shove sent her stumbling forward before she could lay eyes on the person.

Her knees and palms connected with the pavement, the impact sufficient to send waves of pain up and down her limbs and through her body.

Tires screeched, and Nadia turned her head to see a yellow cab bearing down on her as car horns blared nearby.

The cab screeched to a stop inches from her, the cab driver's ashen face and wide, terrified eyes clear through the windshield.

A man in an orange safety vest and tan boots ran to her side and knelt. A white hard hat was all the protection against the rain he wore. "You have a death wish, lady? Jumping in the street like that."

Nadia focused on the man in front of her, the shock of what had just happened, what could have happened, still wrapped around her. She pushed up from the ground, shaky as pain shot up her arms once again. She glanced down at herself, taking stock.

Angry red scrapes covered both palms, and blood trickled from a nasty-looking gash on her left leg. Thankfully, though, she didn't think there was any permanent damage. The same could not be said for her outfit. Dirt and grime covered her dress, and a cursory assessment made it clear that the formerly white coat would have to go in the trash bin as soon as possible.

"You trying to kill yourself or something?" the construction worker asked with a scowl.

Nadia recovered enough to scowl right back. "I didn't jump in the street. Someone pushed me."

The man eyed her with suspicion. "I didn't see anyone near you."

"Well, there was." Nadia scanned the sidewalk. Several people had slowed, some even stopping to gawk at the scene, but in true New York fashion, most walked by without a glance.

An angry car horn sounded.

"Get out of the street, will you?" the driver of the cab that had almost hit her yelled, seemingly recovered from the shock of almost running her down.

Nadia accepted her purse from a gray-haired lady who'd also stopped to help, smiling at the woman. Her umbrella was nowhere to be seen, not that the rain could do any more damage than had already been done. She limped across the street, on the arm of the construction worker, the heel of her left shoe broken. She declined the man's offer to escort her the rest of the way to work. It was only half a block to the hotel, and her appearance would draw enough attention.

She hobbled forward a few steps, then stopped. New Yorkers hurried by as usual. Anyone who'd been around to see her humiliating swan dive into the street had long since lost interest. Yet, the hairs on her neck stood at attention anew. She limped the rest of the way to the hotel, the feeling that someone was watching following her the entire time.

Ryan West declined the coffee offered by Olivia Bennett, Nadia Shelton's administrative assistant, and took a seat in one of two armchairs in the office. His eyes roamed her ground-floor office, noting how much it reflected the woman that worked there.

Bookshelves lined the white walls to the left, while black-and-white photos of the Ponte Vecchio, the Millau Viaduct and the Brooklyn Bridge hung on the opposite wall. He sat facing a white L-shaped desk that sat atop a contemporary area rug, its blue-and-dark-gray hues adding color to the room. Fresh flowers graced a round meeting table tucked into the corner of the office. Feminine, elegant, yet professional, just like the woman who inhabited the space.

He checked his watch: 9:01. Nadia was officially late for their meeting. He moved his neck in a slow circle attempting to release some of the tension there. He'd sent his brother Shawn to get started on the security-system evaluation while he waited for Nadia. It was unusual for her to be late to one of their meetings, but that wasn't why he was irritated. What annoyed him was how much he looked forward to seeing Nadia Shelton.

"Get it together. She's a client."

He was determined to be nothing but professional when it came to Nadia, but a persistent whisper at the back of his mind challenged that determination. He may not have been as personable as his younger brother, Shawn, or as smart as his lawyer older brother Brandon, but he knew the security business. His blood, sweat and tears had grown West Security into one of the East Coast's go-to security and investigations firms.

As vice president of West Security and Investigations, he rarely handled quarterly meetings with clients. In fact, over the last eighteen months, he'd handled only one, Shelton Hotels. Last year their account executive for Shelton Hotels had gone on maternity leave, and he'd temporarily taken on the Shelton. Temporary had turned permanent the minute he met Nadia Shelton.

Their first meeting had taken place in this very office. The memory of her hand outstretched toward him, an intoxicating smile on her face, remained vivid. He wasn't dramatic or even a romantic, but an undeniable electricity had sizzled through his body when he'd touched his hand to hers.

His anxiousness about seeing her grew exponentially in the days leading up to each quarterly meeting. Which was why he was sitting in her office in his best suit, bent out of shape because she was—he glanced at his watch—six minutes late.

He had to turn the account over. He'd been down this road before, with disastrous results to his heart. He didn't even have the excuse of being young and dumb this time. He tortured himself, pining for a woman he couldn't have every time he walked into this office, and it had to stop. He wouldn't jeopardize the company's reputation, or his heart. Not again.

"Oh, my goodness."

The alarm in Olivia's voice had him rising. He crossed to the door but hesitated to open it, debating whether he should stay put or see if he could help. Olivia hadn't sounded like she was in any trouble, and whatever was happening wasn't really any of his business.

A soft voice responded, not Olivia's, but he couldn't make out who it was or what they said. Shadows passed the opaque glass in the office door.

"Should I call an ambulance?" Olivia asked, her voice fading as she passed by the door.

He pulled the door open and followed the sound of the voices to a small restroom at the back of the office suite.

Nadia leaned against the vanity, her dress splattered with mud, wisps of hair falling from her twisty updo. Olivia dabbed at a red gash along Nadia's calf.

A swear rumbled from his chest, drawing the women's attention to where he stood in the doorway. "Get the first aid kit," Ryan ordered, his tone harsher than he'd intended.

He knew they had one. West Security didn't just look out for the physical and cybersecurity of their clients. They made sure the basics that people often overlooked, such as fire extinguishers and first aid kits, were also properly stocked on-site.

Olivia glanced at Nadia with a question in her eyes.

A moment passed before Nadia nodded, and Olivia slipped past Ryan, disappearing down the hallway leading to the public areas of the hotel.

Ryan scanned Nadia from head to toe. In addition to the cut on her leg, she had abrasions on her hands and a wicked scrape along her right elbow. The heel of her left shoe literally hung on by a thread.

"What happened?" He went down on his haunches to examine the cut on her leg.

"I'm the most recent victim of the commuter wars. Someone shoved me into oncoming traffic."

Ryan tensed. "Did you see who did it?"

She shook her head, then winced.

He stood and examined her for bruises before looking into her eyes. "Did you hit your head?" He gazed into her eyes, beautifully dark with flecks of gold. Scrapes marred the smooth umber skin on her arms and legs. Several chestnut curls had broken free from her updo.

"No," she said almost in a whisper, her eyes glued to his. After a long moment, she cleared her throat and looked away. "My hands took the brunt of the fall, but I think I might have jammed my shoulder."

"May I?"

She nodded.

He applied modest pressure along her shoulder and neck, keeping his touch gentle. An intense rush of desire nearly overwhelmed him at the feel of the silky skin of her shoulder. It took everything he had not to keep going when he got to the curve of her neck. He pulled his hand away before he did something stupid. "I don't think it's bad. Tell me exactly what happened."

Nadia pushed away from the vanity and started for the bathroom door. He grabbed her elbow, helping her balance on her broken heel. The scent of her jasmine perfume swirled around him as they walked back to her office, sending another wave of desire springing through him.

"It was probably an accident." Her halting tone belied the words.

"But you think it might not have been."

She didn't answer right away. Lowering herself into the chair he'd been sitting in, she looked up at him through long lashes. "It felt like someone pushed me."

Olivia hurried into the office with the first aid kit, cutting off his opportunity to follow up on what Nadia had just said.

"Thank you, Olivia. I'll be fine. You can get on with your work." Nadia smiled reassuringly.

Olivia shot a curious glance at Ryan. "If you're sure. I can catch up with the other Mr. West and see how he's doing with the security review."

Nadia's smile held steady. "That would be great. Thanks."

Ryan took the first aid kit from Olivia, who shot one more curious look at Nadia before leaving.

Ryan went to his knees in front of her, his six-foot-three height leaving him almost eye to eye with Nadia though she sat. He grabbed an antiseptic swab from the kit and began cleaning the wound on Nadia's knee. He raised his gaze to her face to find her eyes wide. "What are you doing?"

"Can you describe the people around you when you felt the push?" Ryan gently removed her broken shoe, the intimacy of their position sending his heart racing.

"I…I don't know. A construction worker helped me up. And there was an older lady that grabbed my purse for me."

She winced when he brushed the wipe over the wound on her leg, and his gut twisted.

"Sorry."

He wiped the wound again, this time blowing on it gently to minimize the chemical's sting. "Nadia? You okay?"

"Sure. Uh, yes, the construction worker and the lady. There was also the cabbie that almost hit me, but he couldn't have pushed me."

Ryan covered her bruise with a large bandage and moved to the abrasion on her arm. "Do you always take the same route to work?"

Nadia cocked her head to the side. "I live four blocks away. There aren't that many options."

Four blocks. That would put her apartment near Sentinel, the bar he and Shawn had recently purchased.

He finished bandaging her arm. It might be impossible to determine if she'd been purposely pushed or whether some inconsiderate commuter accidentally knocked her into the street, but every fiber in his body wanted to make sure she never suffered another bump or bruise to her beautiful silky skin.

He rose from the floor and stepped back. Nothing could ever happen between them, not only because she was a client, but also because she was way out of his league. That didn't mean he couldn't look and admire how perfectly she was built. Professional or not, he was a healthy thirty-six-year-old man.

His gaze finally landed on her face. For a brief moment, he thought he saw the desire he felt reflected in her brown eyes before she looked away.

Nadia stood and walked barefoot to the other side of her desk. "I need to call the boutique in the lobby and get a new outfit. Maybe you could catch up to Olivia and your brother, and we can talk later?"

He wanted to delve further into whatever had happened this morning, but it wasn't his place, and there wasn't anything he could do about it.

He stole a glance at Nadia as he left the office. She held the phone handset between her shoulder and ear, her fingers punching numbers on the keypad.

*Her fall was probably just an accident*, he told himself as he left the office. Yet, he couldn't stop the thought nagging at him in response.

*But what if it wasn't?*

## Chapter Two

Lana's, the women's boutique in the hotel lobby, skewed toward women with fewer curves and less imaginative fashion sense than Nadia. Since she was in no position to be choosy, she bought a black suit, thankful that it not only fit but covered her bumps and bruises. Paired with an overpriced pair of black flats, she looked the part of a CEO once again.

Unfortunately, the morning's events had put her too far behind to meet with Ryan, leaving her with mixed feelings. She was willing to admit to herself, and only herself, that she anticipated their quarterly meetings with far more excitement than she mustered for any of the other hotel vendors.

Not that Ryan West would ever be interested in the dirty, bruised and disheveled woman that he'd played nursemaid to this morning. The picture of what she must have looked like flashed through her mind, sending a flush of embarrassment through her and heating her cheeks.

She needed to focus on work. She didn't have time for romance, and anyway, given her track record, swearing off men seemed the prudent course of action.

Nadia examined the spreadsheet her CFO had emailed the previous day. Last year's numbers were good, even better than the year before when Nate was in charge. Her father had loved Shelton Hotels, but he'd been slow to change with the industry. As deeply as she'd mourned his death six years ago, when she and Nate took over they'd both agreed that changes would have to be made if Shelton was to survive. Nate hadn't been sure about branding Shelton Hotels as an eco-friendly chain, but once she'd convinced him of the viability of the idea, he'd thrown himself into the rebranding just as she had.

She wanted to take Shelton beyond simply asking guests to reuse their towels and not requesting the bedsheets be laundered every day. They'd instituted a composting program, retrofitted every room in the hotel with automatic lights, changed their cleaning products and completely overhauled how they chose their vendors. It had been a huge and expensive undertaking, but they were paying off the loan right on time. The hotel's margins were tighter than she'd like, but conference season was just beginning, and they were booked solid for the next several months. The only thing missing was Nate.

They'd planned to take Shelton Hotels to the next level together, but now she was left to go it alone.

Nadia's desk phone rang, the caller ID showing Olivia's extension.

"I'm sorry to bother you," Olivia spoke as soon

as Nadia connected the call. "But Michael Dexter is at the front desk asking to see you."

Nadia frowned and for a moment considered having Olivia say she wasn't in. Mike Dexter, president of Aurora Hotels and Suites, was not a man she wanted to deal with today. She'd made the mistake of dating Mike for a short period last year on the rebound from calling off her engagement. Mike hadn't been interested in her solely for her money like her ex-fiancé had been, but it had quickly become apparent his motives were no less selfish. It only took a few weeks of dating for her to realize that he wanted someone who would look good on his arm in public and would fawn over him in private.

That was so not her. Not that Mike had taken the time to get to know her while they'd dated. He'd been too busy trying to impress her and going on and on about how well suited they were for each other since they were both in the hospitality industry. He'd seemed genuinely surprised when Nadia had broken things off with him. The few times they'd run into each other at events afterward, he'd been borderline uncivil. She couldn't imagine why he'd show up at her office.

Today was not her day.

Curiosity won out, however. Minutes later Olivia escorted Mike into the office. With chiseled cheekbones and pale blue eyes, only his relatively short stature of five foot ten set him apart from the many male models that ran the streets of New York.

Nadia plastered a polite smile on her face, rising as Mike entered. "Mike, to what do I owe this visit?"

She didn't offer her hand or come around her desk to greet him. He was more of an interloper than a guest.

"Can't I just drop in to say hello to a friend?" Mike said.

She examined the man in front of her with open suspicion. The quarter-inch strip of pale skin at his hairline announced the bronzy glow on his face as store-bought, and his salt-and-pepper hair fell in waves that were a little too perfect to be natural.

There was no way in the world Mike had come all the way uptown to Harlem just to shoot the breeze. He was up to something, and she'd be wise to tread cautiously until she knew what that was. "I didn't know we were friends. Why are you here, Mike?"

Mike's smile tightened. "I forgot how focused you can be."

Nadia stared and waited.

"Fine." He let the smile drop from his face. "I have a business proposal for you. Aurora is a well-known luxury brand, but we're looking to expand into the midscale market. The board has authorized me to make you a very generous offer."

Nadia cocked her head, suspicion turning to confusion. "What kind of offer?"

Mike pulled a thin white envelope from the inside of his suit jacket and handed it over the desk, his mouth into a grin. "I'm sure you'll be pleased."

She took the offering, sliding the single sheet of paper from the unsealed sleeve. It was a letter, signed by the chairmen of the board of Aurora Hotels, offering a not-insignificant sum for the purchase of Shelton Hotels.

"Of course, the details will need to be worked out, but that's why we pay the lawyers, right?" A new smile slid across Mike's face. "The letter just deals with the important stuff—the money." Mike beamed.

Tension stiffened Nadia's back. She sat. Had Mike been in her office on a personal matter, this would be the point where she would have unceremoniously thrown him out, but professionalism kept her from doing so. "Shelton Hotels is not for sale."

"Why don't you take a close look at our offer before making any hasty decisions?" Mike unbuttoned his jacket and sat in the chair on the other side of Nadia's desk. Stretching his legs out in front of him, he leaned back in the chair, apparently confident that she'd see the light and accept the offer.

Her eyes never left Mike's. "There's no need. As I said, Shelton is not for sale."

Mike straightened in his chair. "I expected a savvy businesswoman like you to reject our first offer. So what will it take?"

Annoyance chased away her earlier inclination toward professional courtesy. "I don't know how to say it any more clearly. I'm not selling Shelton," she said icily.

"What if the deal included a position for you at Aurora? It would be a significant step up."

His rudeness stunned her into a momentary silence which Mike apparently mistook for her considering his offer.

"How does vice president of operations sound?" He smiled a calculated, cocky grin.

"Like a step down from being CEO of my own hotel chain."

Mike guffawed. "Come on, now. Shelton is good for what it is, but it's a stretch to call it a chain. I mean you only have three properties, and they are all in New York. Don't you want more?"

"No." Her hands trembled with contained anger. She was tired of playing his game. And if she had to spend too much longer with Mike and his over-inflated ego, she couldn't promise she wouldn't say or do something she couldn't take back. "But even if I wanted more, it would be here, at Shelton Hotels. The business my father built from nothing."

Mike held up his hands in a surrender pose. "I really didn't come here to argue. I went to bat for you with my board and convinced them that Shelton would be a good purchase. I thought I'd be helping you. Yet, the fact is I've now been tasked with acquiring Shelton, and I don't fail."

Anger surged, threatening to overtake reason. She hadn't asked him to go to bat for her nor could she fathom why he'd think buying Shelton would help her.

Nadia stood. "It's time for you to leave, Mike."

He rose slowly, his mouth pulling so taut that lines

appeared at either end. "Really? You want to play hardball with me?"

Nadia put her hands on her desk and leaned forward. "I'm not playing. Shelton is mine, and that's how it will remain. Now, get out."

Nadia rounded her desk and headed for the door.

Mike stepped in front of her, blocking her path. "Does your refusal have anything to do with our past personal relationship? I know that you might have hoped for something to develop between us, but…" Mike reached out and ran his thumb over her cheek "…sometimes these things just don't work out."

She stepped back out of his reach, her hands balled into fists. "Since I was the one who broke things off, I think I'll survive."

Mike's spine straightened. "I understand it can be difficult to see past sentimentality, but I wouldn't have expected this from you. It's a good offer."

He strode to the door, stopping at the threshold and turning back to her. "Think about it. We'll talk soon."

Nadia watched him disappear.

"Not if I can help it."

## Chapter Three

Nadia's days were usually long, but this day had been longer than usual thanks to her late start and Mike's unwelcome visit. After her busy morning, she'd gotten a good start on closing out the file on the conference of local real estate agents from last week and began to prepare for the conference of freelance photographers that would start early next week. In doing so, she'd been able to avoid thinking about the embarrassment she'd felt with Ryan and the fury that had built from her encounter with Mike.

But as she made the short walk back to her apartment, her mind drifted back to the surprise she'd felt when Ryan had burst into the bathroom. As always, he showed up for their meeting impeccably dressed in what had to be a custom-tailored suit that did nothing to hide the well-muscled body beneath. And she'd been in a torn dress with dirty knees. Still, he'd been exceptionally gentle when he'd lifted her foot from her shoe. There'd been nothing inherently sensual about the act, but it had still been one of the sexiest things she'd ever experienced. And then he'd blown on her calf. It was a good thing she'd been sitting down because her legs—her whole body, to be honest—had instantly gone weak. The last thing she wanted Ryan West to know was that she'd been so attracted to him her knees had gone weak. Having him see her muddy and bruised was embarrassing enough for a lifetime. And a good reminder that she'd sworn off men.

Her choice left her lonely at times, but lonely was a far cry better than heartbroken when the people you loved and depended on left you.

She stood back from the curb while she waited for the lights to change and made it home without a mishap. After collecting the mail from her box in the alcove next to the building entrance, she rode the elevator to her fourth-floor apartment.

She was almost to her apartment door when she noticed it was cracked open.

She crept closer, stopping when a shadow crossed the opening between the door and the frame.

"Did you find anything?" a man whispered.

"There's nothing here," a different, deeper voice said.

"We'll wait for her, then," the first voice responded.

The shadow shifted, and a man in jeans and a black top crossed in front of the sliver of light emanating from the apartment.

She couldn't see a face, but she didn't miss the glint of the silver gun he held in his gloved hand.

Surprised, she let her purse and briefcase slip from her shoulder and land with a soft thud on the hallway carpet.

She crept back, away from her apartment, her keys still clutched in her hand.

Turning, she sprinted back the way she'd come. She couldn't risk waiting for the elevator. She headed straight for the stairs.

The sound of the bar across the door unlatching sounded like a firecracker as she hit it at a run.

*Please don't let them have heard.*

Nadia raced down the stairs, cringing at the sound of her footsteps pounding down the stairs. She'd made it to the third-floor landing when the firecracker sound came again, followed by thunderous footsteps on the stairs above.

*Faster. Go! Go! Go!*

She picked up her pace, unconcerned with the sound of her footsteps now and grateful for the expensive flats she'd purchased earlier in the day.

A sign on the door at the base of the stairs cautioned that an alarm would sound when the door opened. When she pushed through the door and into the alley behind the building, only the usual sound of traffic on nearby Fifth Avenue greeted her. There wasn't time to curse the negligent building management.

She ran for the entrance to the alley. She'd purchased her condo for its location and because of the quiet, tree-lined street on which the building stood. Populated primarily by professionals and young families, the neighborhood offered the serenity and peace she craved after hectic days dealing with hotel guests, vendors and conference-goers. But at ten o'clock at night, the streets were empty, making it impossible to blend in with or hide in a crowd.

*You just have to make it to Fifth Avenue.*

A major thoroughfare spanning a good portion of the length of Manhattan, Fifth Avenue was always heavily populated. There were several restaurants, bars and other venues that would be open at this time of night where she could borrow a phone to call the police.

She ran down the alley. The door she'd exited burst open just as she made it to the entrance to the narrow passage.

She slowed for a moment, glancing over her shoulder. A bald man, almost as wide as the doorway itself, stopped just outside the door. His gaze locked on hers, the malevolence in his eyes visible even several feet away. She attended yoga regularly, but with the fall earlier, her leg muscles already ached and her lungs burned as much as from the sudden exertion as fear. Still, she pushed herself to move faster.

Several people waited yards ahead for the pedestrian walk signal at the corner of Fifth Avenue. Cars streamed down the street.

"Help!"

A car horn sounded, drowning out her cry. The traffic signal changed to red, and the crowd swarmed into the crosswalk, seemingly oblivious to her pounding footsteps behind them.

With a burst of speed, she made it to the corner, sparing a second glance over her shoulder. The bald man still advanced, joined now by another man equally broad shouldered.

Nadia wove through the crowded street. She cursed herself for dropping her purse in her apartment hallway. She could ask to use the phone of a passerby, but stopping to explain the situation would eat up time she could use to put distance between herself and the men after her. Better to get somewhere safe first.

The stores on the block had already closed for the day, but farther down, signs for restaurants and bars still glowed. She kept moving, her eyes locking on a unique sign, its letters illuminating one after the other above a doorway until the name of the establishment glowed in green. *Sentinel*.

It might have been comical in a movie or on television. At the moment it seemed like providence since a guardian was exactly what she needed.

She hurried to the door, pausing at the entrance to see if she was still being followed. The man whose eye she'd caught at the end of the alley skirted around people on the sidewalk. He turned toward her, but she ducked into the bar praying he didn't see her.

Polished chocolate-brown wood covered the walls and climbed to the ceiling where matching beams ran the length of the space. Conversation competed with the pop music falling from the overhead speakers. Bottles of liquor in a rainbow of colors climbed the wall behind the long bar.

People milled throughout the bar, a decent showing for a Monday night, but still far too open to make for a good hiding spot.

The back wall opened up onto a hallway, the universal stick-figure sign for the restrooms hanging overhead. At the end of the hall, a door with the words *Emergency Exit* blocked out in silver lettering beckoned. If she could just get to that door, she could slip out the back and onto the adjacent street without the men chasing her any the wiser.

She weaved through the tables toward the exit, the soles of her flats adhering to the sticky floor.

The door to the bar opened, and her bald pursuer entered. She turned, stepping close to three laughing women headed toward the restrooms. The women shot her curious looks, but she laughed along, the sound brittle. The bald guy would look for a single woman. Nadia could only hope he wouldn't pay close attention to a group of women heading for the restroom.

Their merry band had almost made it to the hall when the door at its end swung open, letting in a chilly burst of air along with one of the men chasing her.

Nadia shifted, moving behind the tallest of the women. She only had seconds before the women turned into the bathroom, and there was no way she could go with them without being seen by the man coming down the hall. If she went in, she'd be trapped.

She glanced back at the front door. The bald man

stood to the side, still scanning the crowd. He hadn't seen her, but it was only a matter of time before he did.

To her left, a corner booth packed with people celebrating something overflowed. Three large men stood around a table, all but masking it from the rest of the bar.

She slid between the two biggest guys and tucked herself in front of one using his body to hide her own.

"Hello." A deep baritone rolled against her back.

Nadia twisted to see the face of the man she was using as a shield, freezing when familiar hazel eyes met her own.

"What are you doing here?"

"I should be asking you that." Ryan cocked an eyebrow at her.

"I…" She stared up at the man she'd been crushing on for the last two years, unsure how to explain why she'd practically thrown her body onto his.

Through the sliver of space separating Ryan and the man standing next to him, she saw the bald man moving through the crowd, examining the women at the bar and at tables one by one.

"I know this is weird, but please don't move. Two guys followed me in here, and I need to hide until they're gone."

Ryan's face hardened. He already dwarfed her, but his body tensed at her words, his broad shoulders expanding.

Having overheard their conversation, the man standing next to Ryan stepped closer, making it harder for her to be seen.

She smiled her thanks.

"This is my colleague, Gideon Wainwright. Gideon, Nadia."

Gideon nodded.

The chatter in the bar was too loud for the other people at the table to have heard her declaration, but it didn't keep them from shooting curious glances at her. A thin man with a wispy blond goatee sitting on the far side of the booth leaned forward as if to direct a comment or question her way.

Ryan shook his head, and the man paused, his lips turning down in a frown, before sitting back in the booth and diving back into conversation with the woman next to him.

"Where are these guys that followed you?" Gideon asked with a Southern lilt that surprised her. With muscles on top of muscles, he looked more Arnold Schwarzenegger than Matthew McConaughey.

"One is a bald guy that followed me in the front door. The other guy came from the back hall."

Gideon angled his body away from Nadia and Ryan, his head turning slowly from one end of the space to the other. Nadia couldn't see the men who'd been chasing her, but based on the hard lines of Gideon's mouth, he did.

"Why are they following you?" Ryan rested his hands on her shoulders. She let herself rest against his warm body. She was still tense and afraid, but less so now that she wasn't alone.

She knew instinctively Ryan wouldn't let those guys get to her.

"I don't know. They were in my apartment when I got home tonight. The door wasn't closed all the way, and I heard them talking about grabbing me. I could see them a little through the crack in the door. One of them had a gun in his hand, so I ran."

Remembering their words and the sight of the gun sent a shudder down her spine.

Ryan kneaded her shoulders. "You did exactly the right thing. You got yourself to safety."

"They're leaving," Gideon said without looking at them. "I'm going to follow them." He walked away without waiting for Ryan's response.

The tension in her body melted away, leaving her feeling like overcooked spaghetti. She would have fallen if Ryan hadn't wrapped his arm around her waist.

He urged her toward the opposite end of the bar. As they moved away, he spoke to the table. "Keep the party going. We'll be back."

RYAN STOPPED BY the bar and asked his bartender, Stacey, to send a cup of hot tea to his office before steering Nadia through a door behind the bar. He'd have asked Stacey to send something stronger, but he wasn't sure if Nadia drank.

"Is it okay for you to be back here?" Nadia glanced back the way they'd come.

He waved her into a small office and moved a stack of papers from a black leather love seat before gently lowering her onto it.

"It's my office. I co-own the bar with Shawn."

He pulled his desk chair across the office to sit in front of Nadia.

Nadia's forehead scrunched. "I thought you worked at your father's security firm."

"We do. The bar is just…" He wasn't sure what the bar was. When the previous owner had decided it was time to retire to Arizona, he and Shawn hadn't wanted to let one of their favorite hangouts close. They'd bought it without a lot of forethought. Lucky for them Stacey wasn't just a great bartender, she was also an excellent manager. "Diversification. Now, tell me about the men that followed you in here."

Nadia crossed her arms over her chest, pushing her breasts together. *Focus.*

"I honestly don't know what they want from me. I've never seen them before."

A knock sounded on the door, and one of the newer waitresses carried in the cup of tea he'd asked Stacey to have sent to the office. He remained silent until the waitress backed out of the room.

"Start from the beginning."

Nadia let out a sigh and explained coming home to find the men in her apartment, being chased from the building through the neighborhood and ducking into the bar. It had been happenstance that he and Gideon had been standing close enough to act as a shield when she'd needed them.

Another knock sounded on the office door. Gideon and Shawn entered without waiting for an answer.

"We followed the guys to a parking garage on

MLK Boulevard," Gideon said. "I thought it would be too conspicuous to follow them inside, but we waited awhile and got the tag of a black SUV that exited soon after the guys went in."

Ryan nodded. "Good. Run it. Let's see who the tag comes back to."

"Already done. Stolen out of Jersey five days ago," Shawn said.

Five days ago. That meant these guys either habitually rode in stolen vehicles or they stole this one in preparation for the break-in at Nadia's. Neither option was good for Nadia.

"Can you think of anyone who might have it in for you? Enemies? Ex-boyfriends?"

His stomach clenched involuntarily at the thought of her with another man.

Nadia rubbed her temples. "I don't have any enemies, and I haven't been on a date in over a year." Her fingers stilled, and her eyes squeezed shut. She clearly hadn't meant to say that last part.

He couldn't stop his lips from quirking up at the news. Shawn's gaze flicked from Ryan to Nadia and back, and Ryan quickly schooled his face.

"Who inherits the hotels if something happens to you?"

She opened her eyes and looked up at him. "It's just me and Uncle Erik, my dad's half brother, now. But there's no way my uncle would hurt me."

Ryan didn't bother telling her what families had done to each other in the pursuit of money. He'd look into Uncle Erik.

"Did you hear these guys specifically use your name when they were in your apartment?" Ryan asked, moving on.

"No, just that they were waiting for me to come home."

So the men might have had the wrong apartment. His gut didn't buy that, though.

Ryan turned to Shawn and Gideon. "Can you two check out Nadia's apartment?"

"No problem," Shawn said.

Nadia slid to the edge of the couch. "Hang on. I appreciate your help tonight, but I can't ask you to do any more. I'm sure my personal security isn't included in the contract you have with Shelton Hotels."

"Don't worry about it," Ryan said.

Shawn's lips curved up in a wisp of a smile.

Nadia rattled off her address and handed over the keys she'd miraculously held on to despite her mad dash through the streets of Harlem.

She stood as Shawn left and began pacing the small space. "Why do you want to check out my apartment?"

"We're not sure who was in the SUV. I'm not sending you back to your place without knowing exactly what the situation is there."

Her laugh was rueful. "I hope you can figure it out because I'm at a loss."

Considering everything she'd been through, she was holding up well, but she'd been operating on adrenaline. That high would wane, and the fall could be emotionally brutal as the reality of how close she'd come to being kidnapped, or worse, began to sink in. It was another reason he didn't want to let her out of his sight.

Ryan leaned back in his chair, rolling it back to give her more space to move the length of the office. "Have you made anyone mad lately? Had a business deal go south?"

"Shelton Hotels has been doing great since Nate and I took over and rebranded as an environmentally conscious chain," she said, pacing again, "but we are small potatoes in the hospitality industry. There's no reason for anyone to come after me."

Yet someone had. Twice in one day. He didn't believe for a second that her tumble into the street this morning was unrelated to the break-in at her apartment tonight. Both attacks were personal, if not well executed, which suggested someone close to her was behind them.

"But you can't think of anyone who might be angry with you or want to get back at you for some reason?" he said to Nadia's back.

She stilled, then turned to face him. "One of my exes came to see me today. Not about anything personal, but he definitely wasn't one of the guys chasing me."

"What's his name?"

"Mike Dexter. He's president of Aurora Hotels and Suites. He dropped by my office this morning, but I don't think he would do anything like this." Nadia shook her head in disbelief.

Ryan jotted the name down. He'd check Dexter

out thoroughly because, while most people never thought someone they knew would target them, he'd been in the security business long enough to know how wrong they often were.

"Mike and I broke up over a year ago." She opened her eyes and looked at him head-on, considering what to say. "Since Nate's death, I've assumed sole responsibility for the company. I haven't had time for a personal life."

West Security had sent flowers when Nate died, and Ryan had gone to the memorial service. Nadia had been the picture of forbearance and graciousness, consoling Nate's many friends. But beneath it all he'd seen the unbridled grief, and his heart broke for her. He hadn't wanted to impose, so he'd signed the condolence book without adding to the throng of people surrounding her.

"I've noticed you've been putting your own stamp on the hotels. Leaning into the green initiative. Making some changes to the buildings. Have there been any employees unhappy with changes you've been making?"

Nadia smiled wryly. "Our employees loved Nate. Some of them preferred his—" she stopped as if searching for the right word "—looser management style to mine. But I can't see any of them attacking me or breaking into my apartment over it."

It was a long shot, but he'd seen people do a lot of irrational things. He wasn't ready to dismiss any potential suspects without an investigation. He asked Nadia for the names of the employees who'd shown unhappiness with her leadership. After a long moment's hesitation, Nadia gave him two names, both assistant managers at the hotel.

Taking over had to have been difficult for her, if only because she'd been thrust into the role of CEO. She'd had to work through the grief of losing Nate and at the same time keep the family business steady. And she'd done it, to all appearances, without breaking a sweat.

But he knew from experience, appearances could be deceiving.

"How are you coping with Nate's passing?"

Nadia plopped down on the couch, her eyes trained on the floor. "As best can be expected, I guess. It was a car accident, eleven months ago. Some days I forget he's even gone, and then it all comes crashing back."

They sat in silence for a long moment. He wanted to go to her, to pull her to him and promise he'd make everything all right. But she'd wrapped her arms around herself, her gaze still diverted from his.

He had the kitchen send a couple sandwiches back to his office, and he was glad to see some of the color returning to Nadia's face as she ate. Not long after they'd finished their dinner, Shawn and Gideon pushed the office door open, forgoing knocking this time. "We checked out the apartment. It was tossed, but I can't tell if they were just being destructive or if they were looking for something. Found this in the hall."

Shawn held her purse and keys out to her.

"Everything's here," Nadia said, relief clear in her voice. "Credit cards, ID and the little bit of cash I keep for emergencies."

Ryan's frown deepened. "So not a straight-up robbery."

Nadia's face paled, and the way she swayed made Ryan glad she was sitting. He rose from his chair and moved to sit next to her on the couch.

"I've got this." Ryan nodded toward the door. It was a terse dismissal, but none of West's operatives were the type to get their feelings hurt easily. Shawn and Gideon shuffled through the door without a word.

Nadia held her head in her hands. "I don't understand why this is happening."

Ryan rubbed circles on her back. "I know. But until we figure it out, I don't think you should stay at your apartment."

She swiped away a tear. "I can take a room at Shelton Harlem for the night."

He wasn't sure that was a good idea either. Whoever was behind this knew who she was, and when she didn't come home, it wouldn't be much of a leap to deduce she might be at a Shelton hotel.

Every fiber of his being told him to take her to his home and not let her out until the threat had passed. The small part of his brain still functioning objectively countered that he was too emotionally involved. Still, his place was a lot safer than a hotel or her apartment. He could remain professional to keep an eye on Nadia.

"You can stay with me. If they know where you live, we have to assume they know where you work."

She examined him with wary eyes. "I don't know."

"I have a big place, and you can't get better security anywhere in the city."

A hint of a smile crossed her lips. "That I believe." Her shoulders relaxed, and a genuine smile transformed her face, making it even more gorgeous. "Okay. Thank you."

"Try not to worry. I promise I will keep you safe."

# Chapter Four

Before heading to Ryan's apartment, they called the police and walked back to Nadia's condo to report the break-in. The officer taking the report wasn't nearly as concerned as Ryan would have liked. She seemed skeptical that the intruders had been chasing Nadia, preferring the theory that Nadia's sudden appearance caused burglars to flee the scene of the crime to avoid being caught. When Nadia pointed out that the men had followed her to Sentinel, the officer had brushed it off as little more than adrenaline-fueled hysteria.

They couldn't prove the guys that had come into Sentinel after Nadia were the same guys who'd broken into her apartment, so there was nothing else they could do except take the officer's card. Ryan didn't even bother to mention to the disbelieving officer that Nadia had been pushed into the street earlier that morning, and Nadia didn't appear to have connected the two events.

He typically used his ride-sharing app to get around the city on his personal time, but he wasn't taking any chances with Nadia's safety. He'd had a company car dropped off while he and Nadia spoke to the officer, and now he navigated the black SUV west to his Riverside Drive apartment building.

He glanced at Nadia in the seat beside him. Her head leaned against the window of the SUV, her eyes closed. She looked tired and scared, but she was still the most beautiful woman he'd ever seen. She was luminous. Not for the first time, he considered breaking his rule about not dating Nadia.

WHEN HE LOOKED at her, he saw a curvy, luscious body, full and round in all the right places. A body he wasn't afraid to admit he'd dreamed about holding on more than one lonely night.

*Get a grip.*

His father, James West Sr., would have a fit if he knew what Ryan was thinking about a client. Shelton Hotels was one of West Security's oldest clients since Nadia's father had signed his first contract with West more than twenty years ago. Back then, his dad had focused primarily on alarms and security cameras for commercial businesses.

Ryan knew his father had hoped that all four of his sons would take over the firm, but James Jr. had decided to pursue a career in the military, and Brandon had earned his law degree. That left Ryan and Shawn, the youngest Wests, to follow in their father's footsteps.

In the years since joining the firm, Ryan and Shawn had expanded the business into a multifaceted, full-service security management firm that handled residential, commercial and personal security needs, as well as investigations of all types for some of the world's most prominent businesses and individuals. They'd also gotten their private investigator licenses and taken on fraud, cyber security and other investigations for their clients.

These days, James Sr. let his sons run the business, preferring the golf course to the office, but he stayed in the loop. More importantly, he held controlling interest and had made it clear that if he thought the boys were on the wrong track with the business, he wouldn't hesitate to take the company away from them. And there was no way their father would see dating the CEO of one of their best clients as anything other than a dumb business move.

Ryan glanced at Nadia again, her chest rising and falling in the steady rhythm of sleep.

He'd keep his hands to himself, but there was no way he'd leave her to deal with whatever this was on her own. Private, round-the-clock security started in the tens of thousands. Shelton Hotels was thriving under Nadia's leadership, but he doubted she'd be able to cover the tab for private security for long. He'd make it work. His brothers wouldn't like working for free, but they'd love having an IOU from him and something to hold over his head.

He turned the SUV into the parking garage under his apartment building. He only lived about a mile from Sentinel, but city traffic was such that even at midnight, a mile drive took longer than he'd like.

He backed the SUV into the space reserved for his unit and shut off the engine.

Nadia didn't stir.

He considered carrying her to his apartment, but after a moment, her eyelids fluttered, and she lifted her head. "I'm sorry. I'm usually better company."

"I'm sure your body needed the rest, with everything you've been through tonight. Come on. I'll show you to the guest room, and you can get some sleep."

He waved a small key fob over the plate built into the elevator control panel, and the button for the penthouse level lit up.

"The penthouse." Nadia's eyebrows ticked up as she smiled. "The security business must pay well."

Embarrassment ticked the back of his neck. West Security was doing well, but that had little to do with where he lived. He'd left the Army and moved back into his childhood bedroom at his father's place. He loved his dad, but that arrangement got old two weeks in. He hadn't cared about the apartment's aesthetics, just that it was his and walking distance from West's Upper West Side offices. He'd given Camille, his brother James's wife and a real estate agent, a budget and his meager must-haves and let her loose apartment shopping. He'd barely looked at the place before signing on the dotted line.

The elevator opened to a stark white hallway with an apartment on either side. Before moving in, he'd run a background check on his would-be neighbor. A pioneer in online gaming, richer than Caesar and a virtual recluse. In the five years he'd lived in the building, they hadn't said more than ten words. The perfect neighbor as far as Ryan was concerned.

The entrance to his apartment contained a small foyer with a long wall blocking the view of most of the apartment.

He tossed his keys into a basket on the table in front of the wall and led Nadia into the main living space. After months of prodding, he'd finally given in to Camille's pressure to let her decorate the living-room space. The outcome was sleek, contemporary furniture with sharp lines and lots of dark leather. Camille conceded to his tastes by artfully arranging a display of art history coffee-table books on the end tables. The overall effect landed nowhere near the rustic feel that he preferred. Since most of his time at home was spent sleeping or watching a game or movie on the big-screen television he'd had installed on the backside of the foyer wall, he hadn't seen the point in paying to have the space redecorated.

Nadia's eyes scanned the large space, and he couldn't help but wonder what the apartment would look like if she lived here. He shook off the thought before it took him to a dangerous place. She was staying with him until he knew she'd be safe, not moving in.

"I'll show you where you'll be sleeping."

He led her past the kitchen area and through the living room to the bedrooms. Despite the generously sized living room and kitchen, there were only two bedrooms, each with its own en suite bathroom and walk-in closet. A king-size mahogany sleigh bed with matching dresser and night tables anchored the room. The claw-foot tub was visible through the cracked bathroom door.

Nadia bit her lip, shifting her weight from one foot to the other. "I hate to bother you for anything else, but I didn't pack any clothes from my place. Can I borrow a T-shirt to sleep in?"

He shook his head, annoyed with himself for not thinking to have her pack a bag. Nadia wasn't the only one who needed to get some rest. "Of course."

Crossing the hall, he pulled a Knicks T-shirt from his bureau and a pair of socks. There was no way she'd fit into his sweats, but the shirt and socks should do for one night.

"We'll figure out the clothes situation tomorrow," he said, handing her the shirt.

"I'll be able to go back to my apartment by then, right?"

If he was right about the events of today being connected, Nadia's pursuers were persistent and determined. That didn't bode well for her being able to go back to life as usual anytime soon. He wouldn't lie to her, but it was late, and they both needed to rest if they wanted to deal with the situation with a clear head in the morning.

Before common sense could stop him, he ran his hand gently down the side of her face. "I don't know, sweetheart, but we'll do our best to get you back in your place as soon as it's safe."

He slid his arm around her waist and tugged her against him.

Nadia peered up at him with wide eyes. He could close the gap between them, just duck his head down and let his lips graze hers. Would she welcome him or think he was hitting on her?

Just the idea that she might think he was taking advantage had him stepping back, his hands falling to his side.

"If you need anything, I'll be right across the hall."

He strode to his bedroom, closing the door firmly behind him and leaning against it.

What was he thinking? She was a client, a client in danger no less. He'd brought her here to keep her safe, not to hit on her. Not only was his behavior totally unprofessional but he didn't take advantage of vulnerable women. He was not that guy.

He pushed off the door and crossed to the king-size poster bed that ate up most of the bedroom. He sat with his back against his headboard and opened his laptop. Shawn had forwarded the information on the owner of the stolen SUV Nadia's pursuers might be driving. The owner, a forty-three-year-old dentist and father of four, had no criminal record and no connection to Nadia or Shelton Hotels that Shawn could find.

He clicked to a second email, this one from Gideon. Still shots from the camera in Sentinel earlier that evening. They had a good shot of the man that had come in through the front door and a not-too-good one of the man that had come through the back. He'd get someone on upgrading those cameras. Gideon's email was one line. *Working on identifications.*

Good. The faster they found out who these guys were, the faster they'd sort this out.

Ryan opened a second email from Shawn. This one contained attachments with background on Nadia and Nathan Shelton.

West routinely conducted background checks on the principals of the companies they worked for. Even though he'd ordered thousands of reports over the years, for the first time he felt uncomfortable reading one, as though he was snooping into Nadia's life.

He pushed the feeling away and scanned the report.

Nadia's father, Calvin Shelton, had worked his way up from porter to general manager at a now-defunct downtown hotel. In the mid-1970s, Calvin purchased the Harlem property that would become the flagship of his small hotel chain.

A marriage in Calvin's fifties produced Nathan and Nadia before his much-younger wife succumbed to cancer. He ran the hotels until his death six years ago. After Calvin's death, Nadia and Nathan took over management of the company. Eleven months ago, at thirty-five years old, Nadia became the sole owner of Shelton Hotels when Nathan perished in a car accident while vacationing in Maine.

Nadia had graduated from State University with

a degree in architecture, which explained the pictures of famous bridges gracing her office walls. She'd also received a certificate in business administration, confirming what he already knew. She was way too smart to be dating him.

His cell phone rang beside him.

"How's it going?" Shawn asked without preamble.

"All's quiet here. Nadia's gone to bed."

"You in there with her?"

"Don't be a jerk."

"Gimme a break, bro. You've had a thing for Nadia Shelton for, like, a year. Now, she's sleeping in your guest room, and you want to tell me you haven't thought about joining her?"

"I do not have a thing for Nadia Shelton." Ryan ignored the memories of almost kissing her that pushed their way into his head. "The woman is in trouble. I'm doing my job."

"Yeah, right." Shawn's guffaw was clear through the phone.

"Did you call to annoy me?"

"No, that was just for fun. Did you get my emails?"

"Looking at them now."

The clicking sound of keys being tapped sounded on Shawn's end of the line. "Sent you a video from Sentinel."

Ryan clicked on Shawn's email. A shot of a tall, well-muscled man, with dark facial hair covering the bottom of his face, filled the computer screen.

He watched as the man scanned the crowd looking for someone.

"The second guy came in the back like she said, but it's not a good shot," Shawn said.

"We need to—"

"I know. Already got a man upgrading the camera. In any event, I didn't recognize the guy we can see clearly. I'll send the shot around the office tomorrow to see if anyone else can get us a name."

"Skip to the stuff about Nathan Shelton."

Ryan opened Nate's background check. Four years Nadia's senior, Nate had graduated from State with a business and finance degree. Despite never marrying, Nate, a rich, good-looking hotelier, had been part of several high-profile, short-term relationships, although he appeared to be unattached at the time of his death. His background check showed a misdemeanor arrest for marijuana possession and an arrest for assault stemming from a bar fight, both from his early twenties. In both cases, the police dropped the charges before trial.

"A couple of arrests twenty years ago. But nothing that would explain what's happening now," Ryan said.

"Keep reading. Miss Shelton's brother liked to keep company with some bad dudes."

The report on Nate was thorough and included information on Nate's close associates, several of whom dabbled in drugs, guns and money laundering, although there was no indication Nate himself had been involved in illegal stuff.

"Notice who's in the picture I included in the report," Shawn said.

Ryan scanned the high-resolution pictures included in the report. Five men stood shoulder to shoulder outside what looked like a nightclub. The report identified each of the men, but Ryan was most interested in the man standing next to Nate. Brian Leroy.

"Nate and Brian Leroy look chummy," Ryan said.

Leroy styled himself as a small-business investor. In reality, the money he invested came from the mob. The owners of the companies that Leroy invested in soon found themselves with less and less control. The few that resisted retirement were met with unexplainable accidents, leaving them unable to work. Or worse.

"It's a place to start. If Shelton hung out with Leroy, there's no telling what he could have been involved in." Shawn paused. "There's no indication that Nadia knows Leroy, but you should find out if she recognizes him."

Ryan fought the urge to bite Shawn's head off. He didn't believe for a millisecond Nadia would get tangled up with the likes of Leroy. But he wouldn't be doing his job if he didn't follow up as Shawn suggested. Even if she wasn't doing business with Leroy, she may have seen him with Nate and know whether the two men had business dealings with each other.

"I'll take care of it," Ryan said. "In the meantime, can you dig up everything you can on Mike Dexter?

And do you think you can work your magic and get me the police report on Nathan Shelton's death?"

"Anything else I can get for you while I'm waving my magic wand?" Shawn drawled.

"That's it for now," Ryan shot back.

"I'll see what I can do. No promises. Why do you want the police report, anyway?"

"Just covering all the bases."

Ryan ended the call and opened a browser window. West paid for several of the top-of-the-line background information programs, but it still paid to do a run-of-the-mill internet search. If people really understood how much of their personal information floated around on the World Wide Web, they'd never touch a computer again.

A search for Nathan's name produced more links than Ryan could read. He scrolled through the list reading the headlines announcing various charity functions and events Nathan had appeared at and donations from Shelton Hotels. It was obvious Nathan enjoyed being the face of Shelton Hotels. There were no hints of Nate being involved in criminality and no other pictures of him with Leroy. But there were a handful of articles about Nate's death. Ryan clicked on one.

While vacationing in Maine, Nathan Shelton's car had plunged off the side of a cliff. The police attributed the accident to driver error, but since the authorities believed Nate's body had washed out to sea, they hadn't been able to confirm. There was a string of related articles linked at the end, most of them about Nate's active social life.

One article caught Ryan's eye. Nadia's engagement announcement. Two and a half years ago Nadia had promised to marry Dr. Wallace Hardee.

A search for Hardee turned up the same engagement announcement and an article about Hardee's work at Mount Sinai's pediatric unit.

A doctor. He seemed like exactly the type of man a woman like Nadia should be with. So why had they split up?

He closed the laptop and tossed it on the bed before striding to the bathroom. He braced his hands on the granite vanity, staring at his reflection.

He'd been close to kissing Nadia, too close. She was a client, not to mention way out of the league of a junior-college dropout. He had to remember that and keep his hands to himself.

There was no question Nadia would be safe from the goons after her as long as she remained with him.

But would his heart be safe from her?

It took some time to fall asleep. When she finally drifted off, she was plagued with dreams of being chased by large, menacing men. A meaty hand had just wrapped itself around her arm when the distant sound of a phone ringing pulled her from the nightmare.

Nadia dragged herself out of bed and into the bathroom. Her reflection was a nightmare of a different sort. Without her sleeping bonnet to protect them, her curls had tangled into a rat's nest. Dark circles loitered under her eyes, and her mouth was as dry as cotton. There was only so much she could do without her usual accoutrements, but a hot shower would go a long way. A shelving unit built into the white-marble vanity held towels, a basket of unopened toiletries and a comb that she used to tame her wild mane.

She turned on the shower and shed her T-shirt. Multiple shower jets, including a rain showerhead, pummeled her tired body.

By the time she finished, she felt human again. She needed a cup of coffee and something to quell her growling stomach, but then she planned to put her mind to figuring out who was after her and why.

She put on her suit from the day before and padded down the hallway. The scent of brewing coffee and cinnamon hit her as she rounded the wall separating the kitchen from the bedrooms.

Her stomach did a flip that had nothing to do with hunger. Ryan stood over the stove, a tight black shirt accentuating massive biceps and jeans cradling a behind that could have been sculpted by Michelangelo.

Ryan looked up from the griddle where French toast sizzled. His eyes stroked her from head to toe, heating every inch of her body. If she didn't know what she looked like, she might have thought the look in his eyes was desire.

"Coffee?" Ryan's husky timber shot through her.

"Yes, please." She ripped her gaze away and headed for the coffee maker.

Coffee in hand, Nadia slid into a chair in the breakfast nook next to the kitchen. She'd barely noticed the apartment the night before, but now she took in the stunning view of the Hudson River from the large window. The apartment was an open floor plan with a large island delineating the kitchen from a sunken living room with its own equally stunning views of the city.

Ryan laid a plate in front of her with triangles of French toast sprinkled with powdered sugar and garnished with fresh melon. He went to the fridge and returned with a jar of maple syrup and his own plate.

She dug in.

"This is great. Where'd you learn to cook?"

Ryan sat across the table. "My mom passed when I was eighteen. My older brothers were off in the military and away at college. Dad worked a lot, so I left school to take care of my younger brother."

"I'm sorry about your mother. And that you had to leave school."

He chuckled. "I did more partying than learning, anyway."

Nadia laughed along with him. "What did you study?"

"Art history."

She raised an eyebrow. "Really."

"Really. When I was a kid, my class took a field trip to the Metropolitan Museum of Art. You know how people say you can go anywhere by reading a book?"

She nodded, taking a sip of her coffee.

"It's the same with art. After I dropped out of school, I got a part-time job with the security company that supplied the guards. Walking those halls sure is something. Almost like being transported to the past."

"I can tell how much you love it. But why choose to work for a security company that wasn't West?"

Ryan paused, his fork suspended halfway between his plate and his mouth. He frowned.

"Sorry. It's none of my business."

"My dad and I didn't always have the relationship we have now. Losing my mother was…well, let's just say it was better that we didn't work together at the time."

"It must have been hard for you to lose your mother at such a young age."

He stared at her, sparking butterflies in her stomach. "It's always hard to lose a loved one."

A familiar pang sang in her heart. She waited until he finished chewing the bite of food he'd just put in his mouth. "I never thanked you for attending Nate's memorial."

Surprise registered on his face.

"You didn't think I noticed you there?" There was no way Ryan West could be in a room and not be noticed by every woman there, but it was endearing that he seemed to have no clue about his draw.

"There were so many people wanting to pay their respects. I didn't want to add to your load."

"You couldn't have."

Their gazes connected. His eyes held hers, not

allowing her to look away. Not that she wanted to. Her heart pounded as if she'd just skied Whiteface Mountain, and there was no doubt in her mind that he knew the effect he had on her.

Ryan's phone beeped, and he pulled his eyes from hers.

She couldn't tell if the message was good or bad from his expression, but she was unprepared for his next question.

"What can you tell me about Dr. Wallace Hardee?"

"I… What?" She pressed a hand to her chest as much to quell the beating of her heart as in surprise. "Why are you asking about him?"

She hadn't spoken to Wallace in nearly two years—nor did she ever want to again.

"You were engaged to him?" Ryan's gaze searched hers.

"Yes, but that was a long time ago." She looked away.

She wasn't trying to hide anything from Ryan, but her relationship with Wallace was a source of humiliation she hadn't totally come to terms with yet. It wasn't as if she'd been a doe-eyed twentysomething when they'd dated. She should have seen the signs he was nothing more than a manipulative gold digger.

"Sometimes anger takes time to build to a place where it gives people the courage to act," Ryan said.

"You don't think Wallace…" She shook her head, her curls bouncing. "No way. I can say without a doubt Wallace doesn't care enough about me to do this."

The raw truth of the statement still stung.

"I want to check him out, anyway. Just to make sure," Ryan said.

Nadia exhaled. "I thought I was in love with Wallace when I accepted his proposal, and I thought he loved me." Bitterness imbued her words. "It took me longer than it should have to realize he only cared about the size of my bank account."

Wallace hadn't even cared enough to call or send his condolences when Nate died. In more than one way she was better off having broken up with him before they'd progressed down the aisle.

"He's an idiot."

She smiled wryly. "I agree."

Ryan's eyes locked into hers again. "You deserve a man so in love with you he burns with it. Who can't make it through a single day without seeing your face. Kissing your lips. Taking you to his bed. Dr. Wally was the luckiest man on earth and too stupid to know it."

Once again his gaze held hers as if it was magnetized. She was pretty sure she'd stopped breathing and would embarrass herself in front of him for the second time in as many days by passing out at any moment.

Thankfully, she was saved by a beep.

Ryan glanced at his phone and typed out a short message. "I need to clean up."

"Right," she said focusing on the remnants of her breakfast until her heart rate slowed. "If you don't mind, could you drop me off by my place? I need to change before I go to the hotel."

His body tensed. "I'll go with you."

"I really do appreciate your concern and letting me stay here, but I'm sure it's safe enough for me to go back to my apartment now." And she needed some time away from him.

Ryan lowered his phone to the table. "I put a couple of men on your apartment last night."

"What do you mean you put men on my apartment?" She sat her coffee cup back on the table with a thunk.

"I was concerned those guys might come back, so I had two of my operatives stake out the building. I wasn't wrong to be concerned."

Fear flowed through her. "They came back." The words were barely more than a whisper.

"They didn't go in. A police cruiser drove by and scared them off. Unfortunately, my men couldn't grab them."

Nadia wrapped shaky hands around her mug, grateful for the warm porcelain against her suddenly ice-cold palms.

"We can pick up some of your things, but I'm not sure it would be safe for you to stay at your apartment until we know more about who's after you. You should also consider avoiding the Shelton hotels."

Nadia shook her head. "I can't do that. We have a conference booked next week at the Harlem property and three weddings this weekend at the Lower East Side property."

The lines on Ryan's forehead deepened along with

the frown on his face. "Couldn't one of your managers handle it?"

She had a great team of people working with her, but she was the CEO of Shelton Hotels. "People depend on me. I have to go to work."

"I'm not suggesting you hide, just that you not take unnecessary risks. Anyone looking for you is going to start at your apartment and the Shelton hotels."

She couldn't hide away indefinitely. Still, she wouldn't dismiss the potential danger she faced.

She drained the last of her coffee. "I'll avoid my apartment and consider whatever you suggest to ensure my safety, within reason."

"*Within reason* meaning you need to go to work?"

She nodded. "Exactly."

Ryan let out a heavy breath and stood. "I can work with that. Let's finish up here and get to your place. I already cleared my day so I could stick with you."

## Chapter Five

Ryan spent the ride to Nadia's condo on the phone arranging for increased security at the Shelton hotels, grateful to have something to do that would keep him from focusing on his almost kiss with Nadia. He'd been attracted to her for months. But hearing how strong she'd been in the face of Dr. Wally's betrayal and Nate's death had shown him a whole new side of her. One he liked. He could fall hard for her if he wasn't careful.

He shouldn't have said those things about kissing her, but he'd been dreaming about kissing her since the first time he'd laid eyes on her. As good as those dreams were, they didn't come close to the real thing. She'd felt so good in his arms. Better than good. It felt like she belonged in his arms.

He slowed the SUV to a stop in front of Nadia's apartment building. He'd had men waiting for them there, so Gideon slid up to the passenger door as soon as Ryan turned off the engine and helped Nadia out of the vehicle. He didn't think it would take too long for her to pack a bag, but he'd rather be safe than sorry.

Dale Jackson, another of West's operatives, slid into the driver's seat as Ryan hopped out, assuming the double duty of staying with the car and keeping an eye out for trouble outside the building. Ryan jogged to catch up to Gideon and Nadia as she unlocked the front door of the building.

Gideon stepped in first and conducted a quick sweep of the small lobby and mail alcove while Ryan and Nadia hung near the door. "All clear."

"This seems a bit excessive," Nadia grumbled as they strode to the elevator.

"Humor me."

Nadia lived in an older, renovated building with four apartments to each floor. The background check he'd pulled on Nadia last night showed she'd purchased the apartment four years ago.

They exited the elevator on the fourth floor.

Ryan grasped Nadia's shoulders, moving her to the side before she could unlock the door. "Let Gideon go in first."

She frowned but didn't argue.

Ryan took her keys from her hand and slid them in the lock. He glanced at Gideon, who held his gun out and at the ready. On Gideon's signal, Ryan pushed open the door. Gideon was inside for several moments before a sharp *Clear* sounded from inside.

Knickknacks, shattered glass and shredded stuffing from the sofa covered the wood flooring. Loose pages from a book scattered about. A general sense of destruction permeated the space.

Gideon stepped back into the hall as Nadia crossed the living room and picked up a picture frame from the floor. A quiet whimper escaped her lips.

Ryan stepped beside her. "Are you okay?"

She looked at him with glassy eyes. "I didn't expect it to look so bad."

Ryan wrapped his arm around her shoulders, and after a brief hesitation, she leaned in to his side. "Why don't you go change and pack a bag."

"A bag? Why?" Nadia lifted her head from his shoulder and looked up at him.

"You can stay at my place until we figure this out."

Nadia eased from his grasp. "I don't know."

"You said you'd follow my lead." He quirked an eyebrow. "Staying at my place, in the guest room, is within reason."

She held his gaze for several long moments before nodding. "There's something else I remembered when we walked in here. I've been getting hang-up calls, and last week someone keyed my car."

"You have a car?"

"I keep it in the garage next door. I don't use it often, but it's useful if I want to get away for a few days." She shrugged. "That's not really the worst of it. Two nights ago I came home to find a mutilated rat on the fire escape outside my bedroom window. I tried convincing myself the neighbor's cat left it, but…"

"Now you're not so sure."

While she packed, he surveyed the damage. Nadia's apartment was an open floor plan, but on a smaller scale than his own home. The kitchen cabinets hung open, the cabinets, drawers and their contents strewn about the kitchen. Ryan lifted a dining chair only to realize one of its legs was broken. He walked through the space, trying to make sense of what they knew so far. Why push Nadia in front of traffic, then break into her apartment, seemingly in an attempt to kidnap her? Was she in possession of something someone wanted, or did they want Nadia herself?

"Ryan," Nadia called from down the hall.

He found her in a small second bedroom that doubled as an office. It looked much like the rest of the house, with papers, books and files tossed haphazardly about the room.

"My computer is missing." Nadia pointed to the white architect-style desk. The power cord remained plugged into the wall behind the desk, but there was no computer at its other end.

"Have you noticed anything else missing?" He took her black travel bag from her hand and hooked it over his shoulder.

She shook her head, sending the loose curls at her shoulder bouncing. "It's hard to tell with all the destruction. If anything else is missing, it's not obvious."

"Anything on that computer worth attempted kidnapping or breaking-and-entering charges?"

"The company's files are kept on a secure server, and I use two-step authentication for all my personal information." She exhaled a sigh laced with exhaustion despite the time of day. "I'll change my passwords when I get to the office, but I doubt anyone could get much information."

Nadia's phone rang. She tugged it from her handbag and connected the call. The color drained from her face as the person on the other end of the line spoke. Nadia sprinted for the front door, the phone still at her ear.

Ryan followed, seizing her arm to stop her from barreling into the hallway. "What is it? What's wrong?"

Nadia pulled her arm from his hand, wrenching the door open with her free hand before turning back to him. "My hotel is on fire."

NADIA ENTERED THE hotel lobby at a run, Ryan at her side.

Olivia stepped away from the two men she'd been talking to when she spotted Nadia coming through the hotel entrance. "Everything's under control. The fire is out, and we evacuated the second floor just to be safe."

Nadia expelled a breath as the claw of tension gripping her neck and shoulders released. No one had been hurt. Insurance would cover any damages.

"Miss Shelton?" The taller of the two men stepped up. "I'm Detective John Parsmons. This is Gene Gould, Fire Inspector." Detective Parsmons gestured to the man that had walked over with him. "The fire has been extinguished, but we will need to cordon off the affected section of the second floor until we complete our investigation."

"Investigation?" Just like that, the claw gripped her shoulders again.

"Yes, ma'am. Unfortunately, it looks like the fire was purposely set in a trash can in the room."

Nadia gaped at the inspector.

"What about the people checked into that room?" Ryan asked.

Olivia shook her head. "That room is vacant."

"Vacant?" Nadia turned her attention to Olivia. "Then, how did anyone get in?"

"The log shows the door opened at 8:43 this morning," Olivia said.

"With whose key card?" Nadia asked, confused.

"No one's," Olivia answered. "That is, the door was opened with a guest key card, but our records don't show a card having been created for that room."

"We'll be investigating all that." Inspector Gould waved away Olivia's words, clearly irritated by the discussion. "Luckily, the people staying in the room next door smelled the smoke rather quickly, and you have a top-notch sprinkler system. The damage is mostly due to water and smoke and is contained to the one room."

Nadia knew the inspector meant well, but she wasn't feeling lucky at the moment. She was thankful no one was injured, but a fire in her hotel, one that may have been purposely started, was not good by any means.

Gould and Parsmons returned to the damaged hotel room. Nadia, Ryan and Olivia headed through the door behind the check-in desk. Nadia headed up the trio through a short hall leading to a small suite of offices where she, Olivia and the hotel department managers worked.

"How many rooms are in the section that the fire department has put off-limits?" Nadia asked.

Olivia sat behind the desk positioned in front of Nadia's closed office door. "Four, but only two were occupied. I've moved those guests to rooms on the fifth floor."

"Great." Nadia chewed her bottom lip. "The first guests for the photography conference will be checking in on Monday. They've pretty much booked every standard room we have. We'll have to move some guests to suites, assuming they aren't all booked too."

"I'll look into it." Olivia spun her chair, so she faced her computer monitor and began tapping away.

"I'll be back." Nadia headed back the way they'd come.

Ryan fell in step next to her. "Where are we going?"

"I need to see the damage."

Ryan put a hand on her arm, stopping her before she could enter the lobby. "It might not be safe yet."

She pressed her lips together, shaking free of Ryan's grip. "I'll be careful, but this is my hotel. I need to know what happened in that room." She was responsible for the hotel, its guests and her employees, and she would make sure they were safe.

He opened his mouth, but she didn't wait to hear what he would say.

Turning, she pushed through the door and into the hotel lobby. She picked up a master key from the front desk, then headed for the elevators, Ryan dogging her heels. With the fire contained to a single room on the opposite end of the floor from the elevator banks, there'd been no need to keep the elevators shut down.

As an enterprising businessman, her father had undertaken a major renovation of the hotel fifteen years prior. Each of the seven floors had been separated into five wings with fire doors between each wing. That, plus the fact that the affected room was at the back of the floor, would make it easier to keep nosy guests from sneaking a peek and getting hurt.

The scent of smoke and burned synthetic materials teased them as they exited the elevator, and it intensified as they neared room 232. Other than her heels squishing into the damp carpet, everything appeared normal from the hall.

She couldn't say the same when she opened the door to the room. "Oh, no."

The inspector said the fire had started in a trash can, but it had quickly claimed the once floor-length curtains which now hung unevenly from a nearby rod. Black marks climbed the wall to one side of the window, and the concrete flooring was exposed where the fire had eaten away at the carpeting.

Detective Parsmons's head snapped up. He pointed the pen he'd been using to scribble notes at them. "Hey, you aren't supposed to be up here."

Nadia squared her shoulders, ignoring the detective. "Have you found any sign of who could have done this?"

"Miss Shelton, we are just beginning the investigation." Detective Parsmons sighed. "Since you're here, are you sure no one checked into this room?"

She narrowed her eyes at the detective. "If Olivia said no one checked into this room, no one checked in."

Parsmons studied her without expression for a long moment. Guilt nibbled at her. The detective was just doing his job; she had no right to take her frustration out on him.

Softening her tone, she added, "I can double-check for you, though."

Parsmons gave her a brisk nod. "Please do."

"Why do you ask?" Ryan said.

Parsmons pointed toward the credenza in the room with the hand holding his small notebook. "There are ashes in a glass over there."

"It's illegal to smoke anywhere in the hotel," Nadia said, the words sounding inane to her ears as she said them. Guests did all sorts of things that weren't permitted by law or hotel policy, smoking the least of them.

"Someone didn't get that message. Look, it's probably just a maid sneaking a puff. Maybe they dropped some ashes in the trash and *poof*." Parsmons raised his hands in demonstration of the fire igniting.

Nadia shook her head. "No Shelton employee would smoke in a guest room."

Parsmons shot her a dubious look but didn't press the matter.

"The fire isn't the only strange thing to have happened to Miss Shelton recently." Ryan eyed the detective.

"Oh?"

Nadia shot Ryan a look that he ignored as he continued to fill Parsmons in on the break-in at her apartment and her tumble into the street.

Parsmons scratched the back of his neck with the pen. "Well, I'll pull the report on the break-in, but I don't see how any of that is connected to the fire."

Ryan's lips twisted into a scowl. "You think it's a coincidence Miss Shelton's apartment was broken into last night, and this morning a room in her hotel was set on fire?"

Parsmons shrugged. "You want me to tell you how many break-ins there were in this city last night? Coincidences do happen."

Ryan's scowl deepened. It was clear he didn't think much of the detective, and Nadia didn't disagree with his assessment. Parsmons seemed ready to blame her hotel staff for the fire, which would no doubt rebound negatively with guests, the media and her insurance company. An insurance company she still needed to inform about the fire, preferably before the detective could poison the well there.

Nadia massaged her temples. "I have work to do."

"We may need to speak with some of your employees," Detective Parsmons said as she and Ryan made for the door.

She turned back to face him. Making an effort to keep the annoyance out of her voice, she said, "Of course. The entire company stands ready to help with whatever you need to complete the investigation."

Olivia's desk was empty when they returned to the office suite. A manila envelope lay on the floor just beyond the door.

Nadia picked it up, her brow furrowing.

"What is it?" Ryan asked.

"Just mail. Olivia usually handles it, but she'll put anything I need to deal with in my inbox."

Ryan took the envelope from her using two fingers. "There's no return address or postage. And I'm guessing Olivia has a key to your office and doesn't need to shove mail under your door."

A weight landed on Nadia's chest at the concern etched across Ryan's face. "She has a key."

"Can I open this?" Ryan asked.

Nadia nodded, her gaze trained on the envelope as if it was a snake readying to strike. Stories about airborne toxins and letter bombs flitted through her mind, but she batted them away.

Ryan grabbed a letter opener and slit open the envelope. A single sheet of paper fluttered onto the desktop where they could both read it.

*WHERE IS NATE?*

# Chapter Six

"This has to be a cruel joke." Nadia looked from the note to Ryan.

Cruel for sure, but his gut told him it was no joke.

"What's a cruel joke?" An older man with a paunch hanging over the waistline of his tailored suit trousers strode into the office.

Nadia turned, and after a beat, her mouth turned up into a tight smile. "Uncle Erik, what are you doing here?"

The man stopped in front of Nadia and raised an eyebrow. "Even though I had to hear about the fire through secondhand sources, I came to see if I could help."

Nadia stiffened. "Things have been hectic here, as you might expect."

Erik's gaze landed on Ryan. "Who are you?"

"This is Ryan West. He handles the hotels' security," Nadia said, her tone strained.

Recognition flickered in Erik's eyes. "West. Yes, I remember now."

"Uncle Erik's accounting firm handles the hotels' books."

Erik pointed to Nadia's desk. "What's that?"

Ryan's gaze flicked to Nadia in time to see her grit her teeth before responding to her uncle. "We're not sure. Probably a prank."

Erik reached for the letter.

"Sir, it's better if you don't touch it." Ryan seized the man's hand before he touched the paper.

Erik shook his hand loose with a glare. "Nate's gone. Why would anyone ask for him?"

Ryan wasn't sure it was a good idea for Nadia to share all that had happened to her over the last twenty-four hours, even with family. Whoever was behind these attacks had gotten into Nadia's home and an unoccupied room in the hotel without raising suspicions. That made everyone close to her a suspect.

Unfortunately, there wasn't time to convey his concerns to Nadia. Instead, he cataloged Erik's reaction as Nadia explained the events of the last day and a half to her uncle. It sounded like something out of a movie—she was pushed in front of the car, chased from her home, forced to face a fire at her workplace and received an ominous and confusing note all in less than thirty-six hours.

Her uncle's expression moved from shock to anger as Nadia finished her recitation.

"I knew this company was too much for you to handle alone," Erik sputtered before squaring off in front of Ryan. "What are you doing to ensure my niece's safety?"

Ryan eyed the older man. Had he been anyone other than Nadia's uncle, he'd have frog-marched him from her office, and they'd have had a long chat about how to speak to a lady.

Possibly sensing the potential for the conversation to head into dangerous territory, Nadia stepped between Ryan and her uncle. "West provides for the hotels' security system, not for my personal security."

"I'll be providing Nadia with personal security until we know what's going on," Ryan said.

Erik held Ryan's gaze, his eyes glittering with anger, along with something else Ryan couldn't name.

"Uncle Erik, do you have any idea why anyone would send me a letter asking for Nate almost a year after his death?"

Erik shuffled his feet and took a step backward. "Of course not. Why would I?"

Nadia took her uncle's hand. "You and Nate were always so close. I thought you might have an idea what all this is about. Was Nate involved in something I should know about?"

Erik's back straightened. He shook off Nadia's hand. "Nate was a brilliant businessman. He'd never be involved with thieves and arsonists. I can't believe you'd suggest otherwise."

Nadia stepped away from her uncle. "I'm not suggesting anything."

"Well, I will not stand here and listen to you disparage your brother." He turned and marched from the office.

"Uncle Erik!"

Erik didn't stop or respond to Nadia's call.

Nadia turned back to Ryan.

Ryan quirked an eyebrow. "Is he always so protective of Nate?"

She massaged her temple. He fought the sudden desire to replace her hands with his lips, soothing away the headache forming behind her eyes.

"Yes. Don't mind Uncle Erik. He's still grieving for Nate. We both are." Nadia eyed the letter on her desk, then moved to the small round conference table in the office's corner.

Ryan wasn't sure Erik's reaction was solely based on grief. Either way, someone believed Nathan Shelton was alive, and he was determined to find out who.

RYAN LEFT TO give the note to Detective Parsmons, but not before making a photocopy and making Nadia promise she wouldn't leave her office before he got back.

Moments after he left, Olivia entered and sat across from Nadia.

"I was able to move the conference-goers we'd planned to assign to these rooms on Monday to another part of the hotel. Can you believe this?" Olivia threw her hands in the air. "Even after the police release the room, it will take weeks before we can use it."

Nadia tapped the pen in her hand against the blotter on her desktop. "I know, but we'll manage. The fire isn't all we have to worry about."

She filled Olivia in on the break-in at her apartment the night before and the note asking about Nate.

Olivia stared, her hand covering her mouth, for several long moments. "This is wild. Is that why Ryan West is here?"

"Yes. He thinks the events are connected and I need protection."

"Does that include what happened yesterday morning?" Olivia said. "I overheard you say you were pushed into that street."

Nadia stilled. "I hadn't thought about it. Yesterday seems like a lifetime ago."

Olivia tilted her head. "It's nice of Ryan to see to your security himself."

Nadia narrowed her eyes at her assistant and friend. "He's just doing his job."

"But you stayed at his place last night?" Olivia shot her a devilish smile.

"Because mine wasn't safe," Nadia shot back. She kept her eyes cast down at the paperwork on her desk, but she could feel her friend smirking. "Don't we have some work to do?"

A knocked pulled their attention to the office door.

Mike stood in the doorway in a gray slim-cut suit that seemed to be in fashion these days. His eyes swept over Olivia from head to toe in blatant assessment.

Olivia's eyes narrowed to slits, her lips curving downward into a frown.

Mike finally turned to focus on Nadia. "I thought I'd drop by and see if you'd thought about my offer."

Olivia shot a questioning look at Nadia.

"And I thought I was clear. I will not sell Shelton Hotels."

"Come on, Nadia. I know your margins are razor-thin. Transforming yourself into an eco-friendly hotel was a good idea, but you don't have the financial heft to pull it off alone in the long run. You need Aurora's backing."

"I don't know what you think you know," Nadia said, "but Shelton is doing just fine. I neither need nor want Aurora's help."

"Fine?" Mike's tone was incredulous. "You can't even keep your staff from setting the place on fire."

Nadia's hands balled into fists at her side. "I don't know where you're getting your information, but the fire was not started by a Shelton employee."

"That's not the word on the street," Mike said.

"Well, I'm here running a business, so I don't have as much time to walk the streets as you obviously do," Nadia spat.

Olivia stifled a laugh.

Mike's eyes darkened. "I'd be very careful, Miss Bennett. I'll be your employer soon."

Olivia's mouth fell open.

Nadia's temper snapped. He'd made his offer, and she'd rejected it. Even if Shelton was in trouble, there was no way on earth she'd sell to Aurora. She'd let her company go bankrupt before she'd let Mike get his hands on her father's legacy.

She stalked across her small office, squaring off in front of Mike. "Get out. And don't come back. Shelton's not for sale."

"You know I never thought you were particularly pretty, but you're actually pretty hot when you get worked up." Mike reached out and caressed Nadia's cheek with his thumb.

Nadia pushed his hand away. "Olivia, call security."

Olivia hurried from the office, leaving the office door wide-open.

If Mike worried about being physically ejected from the hotel, he didn't show it. His presence irritated her, but she couldn't let him know that. He'd use any perceived weakness against her.

Mike leaned in so there was nothing but a sliver of space between them.

She fought the instinct to lean away.

"You know, Nadia, I wouldn't mind seeing you worked up in other contexts. Just because we don't like each other doesn't mean we couldn't enjoy each other. It might even convince you to see reason on this sale."

Mike grabbed her arm and pulled her to him in a quick, practiced move. His lips crashed down on hers, demanding and without an ounce of seduction. He may be used to women who were okay with being manhandled, but she wasn't one of them.

Nadia bought the spike of her heel down on his foot while pushing on his chest with her free hand.

Mike jerked backward, his face twisted in pain, then morphing into surprise.

For a moment, Nadia thought her obvious unwillingness to participate in the kiss had caused Mike to back away. She stepped away from Mike in time to see Ryan spin him around and land a punch to his jaw that sent Mike careering into her desk.

Olivia yelped, moving from her place at the door as Mike pushed off the desk and stumbled toward the exit.

Ryan advanced on Mike with eyes darkened by the fury raging across his face.

"Ryan, no." Nadia grabbed his arm, stopping him from hitting Mike a second time, even though a large part of her supported the effort.

"Who is this barbarian?" Mike yelled. "I want him fired. Now!"

"That's not going to happen. I'm in charge here. I asked you to leave, and you not only didn't leave, you assaulted me. Now, get out before I have you arrested."

Mike swiped a handkerchief over his bleeding lip. "This isn't over, Nadia."

Ryan growled. "Get out of here."

"Not over by a long shot," Mike said, shooting a venomous look at Ryan and Nadia before heading out the door.

"Oh, my gosh. Are you okay?" Olivia rushed to Nadia's side.

The spot on her arm where Mike had grabbed her burned from the intensity of his grip. Ryan's temper looked to be on the edge of detonating, so she kept that information to herself. No permanent damage was done. At least not physically. Mike was not a man that liked to be challenged, especially by someone he didn't consider his equal. If he was determined to purchase Shelton Hotels before this, he'd be obsessive about it now.

"Are you okay?" Ryan's eyes probed hers.

"Yes, yes. I'm fine," Nadia said waving them both off.

"You should call the police and press charges for assault," Ryan said, refusing to be put off.

Nadia rubbed at the headache growing behind her temples. Any other time, she'd do just that, but there were other considerations. An allegation against Mike would bring the press to her door, and with everything else she had going on at the moment, that was the last thing she wanted.

Ryan's expression said he didn't believe it.

"What was all that stuff about? He's going to be my boss?" Olivia asked.

Nadia sighed. She hadn't planned to tell anyone about Aurora's offer. Since there was no way she'd accept it, there wasn't any need to worry the staff. Now, it seemed Mike's visit would make that impossible.

"Nothing. Aurora Hotels has made an offer, which I have rejected. Shelton is not for sale at any price, but Mike thinks he can change my mind." Nadia held up a hand to stop Olivia from speaking. "He's wrong. I will never sell Shelton. I don't want to start a panic among the staff, so Aurora's offer does not leave this office. Got it?"

Nadia looked from Ryan to Olivia. Both nodded their understanding. "Great. We have work to do. Let's get to it."

Olivia left, and Nadia moved behind her desk. Ryan sat at the table on the far side of the office, watching her with an unreadable expression.

"What?" Nadia finally asked on a sigh.

"How did an offer to buy Shelton Hotels end up with the president of Aurora Hotels forcing himself on you?" Ryan asked icily.

She wasn't surprised that Ryan knew who Mike was. There were good reasons West was one of the best. Still, the rancor in his tone shocked her. "That's a bit strong. Mike and I dated briefly. The fact that I broke up with him is probably the primary motivator for his interest in buying Shelton."

"He will not give up easily. Not on getting Shelton and not on getting you."

Nadia stared across the room at Ryan. "Mike doesn't want me."

His expression remained blank. "I wouldn't be so sure of that."

# Chapter Seven

It was already nearing midday, well after the time Nadia usually checked in with her department managers, by the time she finally found the time to do so. She met with the general manager of the Harlem property to debrief the conference that had just ended and prepare for the upcoming one. They also discussed the fire and the workarounds they'd have to make to seamlessly host the events they had scheduled. The conference needed to go off without a hitch, and she had no doubt her team was up for the challenge.

She followed that meeting with conference calls with her general managers at the other two Shelton Hotel properties and a call with her insurance agent. So far the agent seemed nothing but sympathetic and helpful, but Nadia couldn't discount the horror stories she'd heard about insurance companies refusing to pay out claims. All she could do was hope that the police wrapped up their investigation quickly and their results unambiguously showed Shelton was not in any way responsible for the fire.

She and Ryan grabbed a quick lunch from the cafe in the hotel lobby, then she dived into reviewing invoices, preparing the monthly occupancy reports and planning a staff-training session. It was late afternoon before the crick in her neck forced her to take a break. She rolled her shoulders, tilting her head from left to right and back. Ryan worked dutifully on his laptop at the table in the corner of her office.

He'd dressed more low-key than usual today in dark slacks and a formfitting burgundy pullover that accentuated his broad shoulders, powerful biceps and flat abs. As flattering as yesterday's suit had been, she preferred the casual look.

"What are you reading so intensely?" Nadia asked.

Ryan looked up, spearing her with eyes that sent tingles rolling down her spine. "Confirmation on the current whereabouts on your ex-fiancé, Wallace. Seems he's living in Texas and engaged to an oil heiress."

"I guess he'll get his rich wife after all."

"I've also got the background report on Michael Dexter."

She rolled her eyes. "I don't even want to know what it says."

He shot her a crooked smile that added fireworks to the tingles. "It's nothing I wouldn't expect from a businessman that had risen to his position. Some hints regarding questionable ethics on various business deals, but nothing jumps out."

"Mike doesn't like to hear the word *no*, but I doubt he'd go to these lengths just to get me to sell Shelton."

Ryan hesitated before speaking again. "I've also been reading the police report on Nate's accident."

A mix of emotions churned in her stomach. She'd never seen the police report. She already knew more about how her brother had died than she wanted to remember.

"Why?"

Ryan crossed to Nadia and leaned a hip against her desk. "Just trying to get a feel for who your brother was."

Although Nate had been the CEO, Nadia had handled the day-to-day operations of the hotels. She wasn't sure if Nate had ever met Ryan or dealt with West Security, but if he had, his contact would have been minimal.

"That note makes it clear someone thinks Nate is alive," Ryan continued. "We need to know why. And if they're right."

Nadia rose, sending her chair rolling back into the wall behind her desk. She rounded the desk, stopping close enough to Ryan that she had to tip her head up to look him in the eye.

"Nate is dead."

Ryan cocked his head, his expression unreadable. "Someone doesn't believe it."

Nadia sighed. "If you really want to get to know what Nate was like, we should go to his apartment."

Ryan's eyebrows shot up. "I saw that his condo

had been transferred to your name, but I'd assumed you'd rented it out. It's prime real estate."

Nadia reached for the picture of her and Nate on her desk, running a finger over her brother's smiling face. "I haven't been able to bring myself to get rid of his things. And it's convenient for Uncle Erik to have a place in the city to crash if he has a late meeting or doesn't feel like making the drive home to Connecticut." She looked at Ryan. "But that apartment was Nate's sanctuary. If there is something that might help us figure this mess out, it's there."

"I can go by myself."

"No. I want to be a part of this."

She stepped back behind her desk long enough to pull her purse from a drawer.

It was after five; the evening shift had already clocked in, and Olivia had headed home. Nadia locked her office, and they headed for the garage next door where Ryan had parked his SUV earlier that morning.

Ryan pointed them south to Nate's Upper East Side condo, fighting rush hour traffic the whole way.

Nate's building was architecturally more similar to Ryan's than hers. The thirty-three-floor high-rise possessed all the amenities a rich bachelor could want: on-site cleaners, concierge, maid service, spa and gym. Twenty-eight floors above the city, the condo boasted spectacular views, despite being relatively small. A galley kitchen jutted off to the right of the entrance and looked into a decent-sized dining–living room combo. A black bookshelf held a smattering of books and several framed pictures of Nate with prominent people. The mayor. A city councilman. Even a United States secretary of state.

A narrow hall opened up beyond the living space.

"Nate used the second bedroom as his office. I think we should start looking there for…" she threw her hands up "…whatever we're looking for."

Ryan followed her down the hall and into the bedroom the office. The room's sleek black-and-silver decor, minimalist and masculine, was all Nate. A sleek arched-legged desk occupied one corner, flanked on either end by more black bookshelves. A metal file cabinet stood in the adjacent corner.

"Do you mind if I see what's in here?" Ryan asked, pointing to the file cabinet.

Nadia's chest rose and fell with a shuddered breath. "I guess that is what we're here for."

She crossed the room to the desk while he turned to the cabinet. Sitting at Nate's desk, she let her gaze linger on a photo of the two of them at one of the rare charity functions where he'd felt they both needed to make an appearance. One of the last times she'd seen him.

She turned away from the photo and booted up Nate's computer. It was only the second time she'd been in Nate's apartment since his death but the first time she'd ventured into his office, a place Nate had rarely let anyone in. She could have sworn the space still smelled faintly of her brother's favorite cologne, though common sense told her that wasn't possible. An acute stab of grief rippled through her.

Shaking off as much of her melancholy as she could, she was for once thankful that he never listened to her about the danger of using a combination of their mother's name and their childhood address as his password. She scrolled through the files on the laptop not sure exactly what she was looking for. The file labeled *Bronx Project* both surprised and annoyed her.

She and Nate agreed never to keep company files on their personal computers. Having files spread over multiple devices not only made it difficult to keep track of them, but it also made it more likely sensitive company information could fall into the hands of a competitor.

"Humph."

Ryan turned at her exclamation. "Did you find anything?"

"Nothing that helps us. It looks like Nate was inquiring about buildings for sale in the Bronx. He never mentioned an interest in purchasing a new property to me." She didn't bother masking her irritation.

Ryan crossed the small room and looked over her shoulder at the computer screen. "Maybe he hadn't gotten around to talking to you about it."

"You're probably right." Nadia turned in her chair to look up at him. "Did you find anything?"

Ryan shook his head. "Just the usual personal papers—copies of past tax returns, the deed to this place, insurance papers."

She sighed. "I probably should have known that.

Uncle Erik was Nate's executor. He handled everything after Nate died. For a while, I could barely keep it together enough to handle the hotels."

Ryan laid a hand on her shoulder, which she covered with her own. "That's understandable."

When she'd come to the apartment with Uncle Erik, he'd been all business, hustling her in and out as quickly as possible. Maybe he thought it was the only way for them to get through being in Nate's space. But now new waves of grief for her brother washed over her, and she let herself feel them. Eventually, she'd have to get rid of Nate's things whether she rented the place or sold it, which would be yet another reminder that he was never coming back.

She leaned into his hand. He ran his thumb in soft circles over the swell of her cheek.

"Are we done? I've had enough memories for one day." She turned her back to Ryan, not wanting him to see the tears threatening to fall.

He stepped back, his hand falling from her shoulder. "I want to take a quick look in the bedroom."

She powered down Nate's computer, and they crossed the hall.

Nadia opened the bedroom door and screamed.

Ryan swore, reaching for the gun at his back, as he turned her away from the sight of the dead man on the floor, his sightless eyes staring at the ceiling.

## Chapter Eight

The first officer to arrive took Nadia's and Ryan's statements, then ordered them to remain in the hall outside the apartment. They didn't wait long before Detective Parsmons arrived. He eyed them and went into the apartment without stopping to speak. Nearly an hour passed before Parsmons came back out with another man that he introduced as Detective Beard.

Detective Beard led Ryan to the opposite end of the hall to talk, while Parsmons asked Nadia to go over the events of the evening for him.

Exhaustion clutched at her despite the relatively early evening hour. Still, Nadia repeated the statement she'd given the officer when he'd arrived.

"Walk me through it again," Detective Parsmons said when she finished, peering at her over round-rimmed spectacles.

She sighed heavily, fighting the urge to slide down the wall and sit. Her legs felt ready to give out.

"I told you. We came by the apartment to see if we could discover who might be behind all the things that have happened to me."

"And you came straight here from the hotel?"

"Yes. I was at the hotel all day."

Detective Parsmons looked down at the notebook in his hand. "And when you got here you went straight to the office? You didn't stop by the bedroom first?"

"No," Nadia said through gritted teeth. "The office seemed to be the most logical place to look first."

"Humph." Parsmons didn't look up from his notes. "Then what?"

For the second time, Nadia took him through the course of events, starting with finding nothing helpful in the office, then moving to the bedroom and discovering the dead man.

"Who has keys to the apartment?" Parsmons asked.

"My uncle and I. He stays here sometimes when he doesn't want to make the trek back to his house in Greenwich."

"But the place is in your name, right? So legally it's yours?"

Nadia rubbed her brow, warding off the headache growing there. "Yes, but this is the first time I've been here in months."

"Humph," Parsmons repeated.

"It's been a long day." Ryan's familiar deep voice came from behind Nadia, just before she felt his hand on her back. "If you're finished with your questioning, I'd like to take Nadia home."

Relief flowed through Nadia.

Detective Parsmons's eyes shifted to Ryan. "One

more question. Either of you have any idea who the dead man is?"

"No," Ryan said.

At the same time, Nadia answered, "Yes."

Nadia shifted as Ryan and Parsmons looked at her with twin expressions of surprise.

"I don't actually know the man, but he looks like one of the guys that chased me into Sentinel last night."

"But you didn't recognize the dead guy?" Parsmons directed the question to Ryan.

Ryan frowned. "No, but I was focused on Nadia." Ryan tapped the screen on his phone. "I pulled the footage from Sentinel's cameras." He turned the phone so they could all look at the video. "He could be the dead guy."

Ryan pointed to the man that had come in through Sentinel's back door.

"Can you send me that video?" Parsmons asked, handing Ryan a business card.

Ryan tapped the phone screen a few more times, then tucked the phone into his pocket.

Parsmons snapped the leather cover on his notebook closed. "You know I find this all very peculiar, I have to say. There's a fire in your hotel, and a suspicious note is left in your office. And now the man you say broke into your home and attempted to kidnap you is found in an apartment you own."

Ryan's arm slipped around Nadia's shoulder, pulling her into his side. The warmth of his body radiated through her. "If you've got something to say, spit it out, Detective," Ryan growled.

Parsmons's eyes narrowed and swung from Nadia to Ryan and back. "Okay. You, Miss Shelton," Parsmons said, pointing to Nadia, "have access to all the relevant places in this story. Your apartment. This apartment. The hotel. You seem to be the common denominator. Why is that?"

Nadia stiffened but held Parsmons's gaze. "I don't know, Detective."

"Me either." Parsmons pointed his index finger at her. "But I'm going to find out."

SHE WAS MORE than ready to leave Nate's apartment once Parsmons released them. She didn't want her Uncle Erik to hear about the dead body found there from someone else and worry, so she called him as soon as she got back to Ryan's apartment.

"Are you okay? Tell me where you are. I'll be right there." Her Uncle Erik's voice boomed from the other end of the phone.

Nadia glanced around Ryan's guest room. She wasn't about to tell her uncle she stayed the night with a man she barely knew. He'd have a heart attack. She couldn't explain it, but despite only knowing Ryan through his security work with the hotel, she knew without a doubt she was safest with him.

"Don't come back into the city. You don't have to worry about me. I'm staying the night with a friend. I just wanted to warn you that the police will probably be in touch and Nate's apartment will be off-limits for a while."

"Well, for how long?"

Nadia clenched her teeth. "I don't know, but while the police are investigating, you can take a room at one of the hotels if you're going to stay in the city."

"It's not that. I was going to call you. I have to go out of town for a day or two."

"Something serious?"

"No, no. An issue with a client that has to be dealt with in person."

Nadia promised to keep him updated before ending their call and exhaling deeply. She fell back onto the bed, her legs dangling over the edge, and took a moment to simply feel the soft mattress at her back and enjoy the quiet. Uncle Erik was tightly wound by nature, and conversations with him were often energy sucks. Given where her energy meter had been when she'd initiated the call, she was now running on fumes.

She was debating whether to just call it a night and slide under the covers when the smell of onions and ginger snaked its way under the door, making her stomach grumble. She climbed off the bed and made her way to Ryan's kitchen.

Ryan spooned chicken stir-fry onto two plates. "I figured you'd be hungry."

"You were right," she said as Ryan brought their plates to the table. "This looks great. Thanks."

Ryan sat opposite her at the table but didn't begin

eating. "It's not every day you find a body. How are you doing?"

She wasn't sure how to answer that. Finding a dead man's body in Nate's apartment had been a shock on top of all the other emotions that had swelled inside her from being back in her brother's personal space. Now, she just felt worn down, and she couldn't wait until she could fall asleep.

"As well as can be expected, I guess."

They ate in comfortable silence for several long moments.

"I have to take a day trip to Maine tomorrow. I've arranged for one of our best men to stick with you while I'm gone," Ryan said.

"What are you going to do in Maine?" she asked, although she thought she already knew the answer.

Ryan held her gaze. "I want to talk to the sheriff that investigated Nate's accident."

"Why? You read the report. What more do you need to know?"

Ryan hesitated before speaking. "The report is the official record, but it doesn't tell me anything about the investigating officer's opinions and gut feelings. I'm much more likely to get that out of the sheriff if I speak to her in person."

She shook her head. "I don't know what you think you'll find."

"Maybe nothing, but part of the reason I'm good at my job is that I'm thorough. I'll be back tonight."

"I'm going with you." Nadia wiped her hands on the cloth napkin next to her plate.

Ryan frowned. "That's not necessary."

"It absolutely is. You obviously think something Nate was into before his death could be the key to what's going on here. I don't know that I agree with that, but I trust you. And if you're right, I want to know what that is."

Nadia waited without breaking eye contact while Ryan silently assessed her. She was involved in this, whether she wanted to be or not. She would not sit back and play the damsel in distress, leaving Ryan and West Security to crack the case.

"Okay. We'll be leaving at six. It's a little over a three-hour drive to Northpath, Rhode Island. I'd like to talk to the sheriff and be back on the road to New York before the sun goes down," Ryan finally agreed.

They fell quiet once more as they finished their dinner.

This time, Nadia broke the silence. "I love your view."

Through the floor-to-ceiling windows, she could see the lights of New Jersey across the Hudson River.

Ryan shifted his seat, putting his chair closer to Nadia at the same time. "I let my sister-in-law do most of the house hunting, sifting through all the condos on the market and all those viewings. I just chose from their top three, and the view out that window is what won me over."

"Wow. That's…efficient."

Ryan chuckled. "My needs are minimal. A large wall for the flat screen, a decent kitchen and a nice big tub are all it takes to make me happy."

Her stomach clenched as an image of Ryan in a tub lodged itself in her head. She wouldn't have pegged him as someone who'd prefer soaking over showering, but now that he'd mentioned it, she couldn't stop imagining him in the bath.

"It reminds me of this cabin in Maine my parents used to drag my brothers and me to every August," Ryan said, pulling out of her fantasies.

"You might be the only person to look out a New York City window and see Maine."

"It's the water and the lights. The cabin was on a hill next to this huge lake. It overlooked the town below, and at night I loved to sit out on the deck. I used to make up stories about what the people in all the houses below ours were doing. Always something cooler than daydreaming on the front porch."

"It sounds wonderful. My family used to go down South to my aunt's house in Atlanta for our family vacations. After my mom died, we stopped going. Kind of lost touch with that side of the family."

Aunt Celia had passed away when Nadia was a teenager, and now she had cousins she wouldn't even recognize. Since their father's passing, it had been her and Nate against the world. And now she was on her own.

She shook off the gloominess threatening to engulf her. She had Uncle Erik. They didn't see eye to eye on many things, but he was always there for her.

Nadia stole a glance at Ryan. When she'd needed him, he'd been there for her.

"You didn't take any vacations after your mother died?" Ryan asked, pulling her from her thoughts.

Nadia shrugged, swallowing the last of her dinner. "Dad worked a lot building the business, and once Nate and I were old enough, we also worked at the hotel. My father believed we should have a thorough understanding of the business we'd inherit someday, so I've pretty much worked every position we have at Shelton Hotels."

Ryan cocked his head to the side. "I'm trying to imagine you in a maid's outfit."

Heat flooded every inch of her body.

Ryan's face colored. "I'm sorry. I shouldn't have said that," he said, rising with his plate.

"It's fine." It was more than fine. The image stirred a desire in her that threatened to overwhelm her. And the knowledge that Ryan was attracted to her sent a surge of feminine confidence through her that she hadn't felt in a very long time.

"No, it's not. It was unprofessional." His plate clattered into the sink.

She followed him, carrying her plate. "It's not like I'm paying you," she said, attempting to lighten the moment.

When it didn't work, she moved on to something that bothered her.

"I know you said not to worry about it, but I want you to bill me for the personal security. I might need to work out a payment schedule, though." Nadia laughed, only half-kidding.

"Stop." Ryan faced her, his tone still sharp. "I told you not to worry about it, and I meant it."

She frowned, her annoyance growing. If he thought she would lose her head over one flirty comment, he could just get over himself. "Why? I know Shelton has been a client for years, but you barely know me. Why would you help me for free?"

"Why? Because every time I see you, it gets harder and harder to resist doing this."

He stepped forward, closing the space between them. Wrapping an arm around her waist, he pulled her tightly to his chest. The scent of his spicy cologne filled her senses. He dropped his lips to hers, and she gasped at the warmth of his mouth on hers.

She relaxed into the kiss, and he pulled her closer, his mouth moving against hers in a slow, seductive dance. His tongue stroked hers, sending heat spiraling through her body. She moaned and slid her hands over the coarse hair on his chest and around his neck, drawing their bodies closer, fixing her hips to his.

Ryan groaned deep in his chest and lifted her, sitting her on the countertop and stepping between her legs.

His cell phone vibrated, breaking the spell they'd been under.

He jerked away as if the touch of her lips had scalded him. His eyes were a storm of emotion as they held each other's gaze through two more rings before he tore away to look at his phone.

"I've got to take this." He answered the call, leaving the kitchen without looking back at her.

Nadia walked hurriedly to her bedroom. Hot tears stung her eyes. Ryan clearly thought their kiss was a mistake. She shouldn't let it bother her. They had a business relationship and nothing more. Adding a personal relationship to the mix right now was beyond unwise.

So why did she feel like she'd lost something she just realized she wanted?

# Chapter Nine

Ryan stood in the kitchen at five fifteen the next morning. His cell jiggled on the countertop, and he looked down to see Shawn's face staring up at him from the phone's screen.

He pressed the button to start brewing coffee before connecting the call. "What's up?"

"Dead guy's name is Andrei Ledebev," Shawn began without preamble. "He and his brother, Taras, are new to the New York scene, but they're well-known in other illegal circles. They've been working with Brian Leroy."

"That's not good."

"No, but this is worse. Leroy appears to be working with Lincoln Smith."

The real mob families looked nothing like the one-note portrayals given in the movies with shakedowns at the neighborhood mom-and-pop stores. In reality, organized crime had stepped into the twenty-first century with everyone else. Today's gangsters had college degrees, wore three-thousand-dollar suits to the office and were more diverse and gender-balanced than the average state legislature. Greed knew no ethnicity, and mobsters like Lincoln Smith would work with anyone who could make them money.

New York organized-crime families, in particular, had their hands in a wide variety of cookie jars, many of them quite legal, at least before the mobsters got their hands on them. Leroy was ostensibly a well-known small-business investor, but in reality, he was simply a well-educated and sophisticated loan shark. Aligning himself with Smith was a step up on the metaphorical crime ladder from the crew of misfits Leroy had run with in his youth.

"That is not good, but it is a link to Nate," Ryan said, putting four pieces of toast in the toaster.

"So Leroy or Smith could be behind the attacks on Nadia, but why?" Shawn asked.

"If we can figure out the relationship between Nate and Leroy we might answer that question. Has Eugene been able to get anything from the cameras at Shelton?"

He'd asked Eugene Paul, head of West's technology and communications department, to look at the security-camera footage from the hallway of the room where the fire had been started. He'd viewed the security tape himself, but whoever set the fire had kept his head down and face obscured. It hadn't helped that the cameras weren't the top of the range that West Security offered its customers. That was a problem Ryan had promptly fixed, ordering all the cameras in each of the three Shelton properties be upgraded and the bill directed to him. The IOUs he'd owe his brothers were adding up quickly, but as long as Nadia was safe, he'd happily pay them.

"He's working on it, but I wouldn't get my hopes up," Shawn responded.

"Tell him to keep at it and take a look at all the other footage of the hotel around the same time."

"Do you know how much time that could take?"

"I know, I know, but have Eugene do it, anyway. Something about that fire isn't right." Ryan rubbed the back of his neck.

"What do you mean, *isn't right*?"

"If I knew, I'd tell you. Just have Eugene do it as soon as he can." He looked over as Nadia entered the kitchen. "I gotta go."

Her forest green top grazed the top of the black jeans that hugged her hips. The outfit wasn't overtly sexy. Still, he couldn't tear his eyes from the way her hips swayed as she crossed the kitchen toward him, the steady rhythm of her low-heeled boots contrasting with the erratic beat of his heart.

She stopped at the edge of the counter, several arm lengths away from him. Her expression was blandly polite, revealing nothing of what she thought about the kiss they'd shared the night before.

"I made toast for the road. You can put your coffee in this and take it with us." He took a thermos from an upper cabinet and handed it to Nadia.

"Thanks." Nadia took the thermos and turned away from him.

He waited until she'd filled it and buttered her slices of toast. "You ready?"

"Sure." She turned for the front door without a backward glance.

A sigh escaped his lips. This was exactly why he'd sworn he wouldn't cross the professional line with Nadia. Then he'd not only crossed it, he'd leaped over it with abandon. If this road trip was uncomfortable, he had only himself to blame. Still, better that he endure an uncomfortable road trip than another broken heart.

Nadia's phone rang before she made it to the door. She glanced at the screen and groaned.

"What is it?" Ryan said.

"Uncle Erik. I left him a message telling him that we're going to Rhode Island." She silenced the phone and slipped it in her coat pocket. "I don't have to speak to him to know what he'll say. Let's go."

Dawn bloomed as they drove out of the city in silence. His GPS put the trip at three and a half hours. Nadia spent the first hour and a half studiously looking out of the passenger window.

He pulled into a rest area, more because he needed a break from the tension in the car than anything else.

"I'm going to grab a coffee and maybe a breakfast sandwich. Do you need anything?"

She studied the cars out the passenger window as if there'd be a quiz later. "No. I'll just wait here for you."

He pushed his door open, then slammed it shut

again causing Nadia to start and face him for the first time since they'd gotten into the car. "Look, I'm sorry about last night. I shouldn't have kissed you."

"It's fine." Nadia twisted, so she looked out of the window once again.

He started to reach across the console for her hand, then thought better of the move. He wanted to repair the damage he'd done, not send mixed signals. "Nadia, please look at me."

She didn't react at all for several long moments. Finally, she faced him. "I get it. You made a mistake, and it won't happen again. You don't have to worry about me complaining to your father or suing or whatever."

His stomach clenched at the pain he saw in her eyes. "I'm not worried about you suing, and I don't think kissing you was a mistake. I've been thinking about kissing you for months."

Her expression read of disbelief, and he didn't blame her for her suspicion.

"It was unprofessional to have kissed you. Now is not a good time for me to be distracted. Not when all my focus needs to be on keeping you safe."

The suspicion in her eyes turned to anger. "Well, I'm sorry I'm such a huge distraction." Nadia reached for the car door handle.

This time he did take her wrist, stopping her before she could exit from the car.

"That's not what I meant." He released her wrist and scrubbed his hands down his face. "Look, I'm attracted to you. I think you're attracted to me too, even though you look like you want to rip my head off. Right now you need someone focused on protecting you and figuring out who is behind all the things that have been happening to you lately. I can't be that person if I'm wondering when I'll get to kiss you again."

Nadia held his gaze for several long moments before her shoulders straightened and drew back. "You're right. We should keep things professional. Friends?"

She extended her hand.

Friends was the last thing he wanted to be, but he took her hand. Ignoring the electricity jolting through him at her touch, he said, "Friends."

They strode into the rest stop together. Nadia allowed him to pay for her breakfast, which he took as a good sign. They ate quickly and were back on the road to Rhode Island forty minutes after they'd stopped.

They hadn't made it far from the rest stop when his GPS alerted to a traffic accident backing up the interstate up ahead. He followed the mechanical voice directing him onto a two-lane state road. It would add a bit of time to their trip, but the road was lightly traveled.

"So West identified the dead man in Nate's apartment." Ryan shot a glance at her across the car. He hoped opening up about the state of the investigation would help to put them back on a sound footing.

"I overheard you on the phone this morning." She

sipped the orange juice that had come with her break-fast sandwich.

"Have you ever heard the names Taras or Andrei Ledebev?"

Creases formed on her forehead. She considered his question for nearly half a minute before answering. "I don't think so. Is one of them the dead guy?"

"Andrei. But both worked for Brian Leroy."

Nadia scowled. "Leroy's construction company bid on one of our renovation projects a couple of years back. But Leroy wouldn't do all this just because we didn't use his company."

"No, but there's evidence that Nate and Leroy had a relationship that went beyond business. At least one event that they were both in attendance at and pho-tographed together."

"That doesn't mean anything."

They'd just gotten back on speaking terms. He didn't want to rock their precarious boat, so he let the subject drop.

In the rearview mirror, he watched as a black pickup truck behind them accelerated. The road had narrowed into one lane in each direction, but they were the only two cars present at the moment.

The pickup rode their bumper. Despite the danger-ous proximity, Ryan wasn't able to get a good look at the driver through the dark tint on the windshield.

Ryan sped up.

The SUV followed suit.

"Someone is tailgating us." He glanced at Nadia. "Make sure your seat belt is on and tight."

Nadia twisted so she could see the car behind them. "What is he doing?"

"Can you see who's in the car?" He pushed the accelerator to the floor, but the truck picked up speed along with them.

"No. The window is too dark."

The SUV rammed the back of their vehicle. Nadia jerked forward as the car slid, fishtailing, but Ryan kept them on the road. He guided the car out of the skid and revved the engine, sending them flying forward.

The SUV sped up, hitting them again and sending Nadia crashing into the dashboard.

"Nadia! Are you okay?"

She groaned. He risked a glance at her. Blood trickled from a gash on her forehead.

"I think so," she said.

The SUV hit them again, sending them into a tailspin.

Ryan fought to regain control of the car, but the tires slipped off the road and down an embankment.

Brush flew by as he pumped the brakes trying to slow the car. Several large oaks at the foot of the embankment loomed. He wrenched the wheel to the right moments before the sound of crumpling metal filled the air.

"Ryan!"

He swallowed a curse and reached across his torso, touching his hand to the site of the pain. A shard of glass from the shattered window left a deep gash above his hip. His fingertips were bloody when he pulled them away.

"I'm okay. How about you?"

"A bump on the head, but nothing to worry about." Nadia turned in her seat. "The back windshield is shattered. I don't see anyone."

"That doesn't mean they aren't there. We need to get out of this car." He reached for the seat belt release and groaned. He spent the next several moments concentrating on breathing through the searing pain in his side.

"You shouldn't move." Nadia pulled her phone from her purse at her feet and dialed 9-1-1.

She gave the operator their location and relayed a description of the car that had driven them off the road.

He fought through the pain and reached into the glove compartment, taking his gun from inside. They may not be able to get out of the car, but he would not let them be slaughtered like sitting ducks either. He rested the gun on his thigh, within arm's reach, as they waited for help to arrive.

The sound of sirens swelled nearly ten minutes after they'd landed in the ditch.

"Put this back in the glove box." He held the gun butt-first out to Nadia.

She recoiled as if the gun would bite. "I don't like guns."

He shot her a smile, twisted with amusement. "I'm not asking you to shoot it. Just put it back. This will go a lot smoother if it's locked away when the cops arrive."

The cops might still have questions for him, but since he had a license to carry, he doubted they'd give him trouble.

On the way down, in a car that refused to stop, it had seemed as if they were falling a hundred feet down a steep incline. Now, Ryan could see that they'd only slid about ten yards from the road, down a slight slope. He ignored the pain in his side and gave a statement to the deputy who followed them up the incline.

Two ambulances waited at the top of the incline.

Ryan lowered himself onto a stretcher with the help of the EMTs. "We need to ride to the hospital together."

The bleeding from the cut on his side had subsided, but it still burned like the devil himself walked across his torso whenever he moved.

"Sorry, sir. Space won't allow two stretchers."

He didn't want to leave Nadia's side. Yet, he could barely sit up, and he wasn't going to take any chances that Nadia's bump on the head wasn't something more serious. He called out to the deputy that had taken his statement and explained that there had been several attempts to harm her. The deputy promised someone would stay with Nadia at all times.

It wasn't as good as having her by his side, but it was the best he could do at the moment. Still, if forcing them off the road was an attempt to separate him from Nadia, her assailant had just gotten exactly what he wanted.

The victims from the five-car pileup that caused him to turn off the interstate in the first place were also being seen at the hospital. Unfortunately, several people involved in that accident were in critical condition. The deputy kept his word, thankfully, and had an officer shadow Nadia while the doctors examined her head wound.

Ryan called Shawn and filled him in while he waited to be seen by the doctor. He wasn't surprised when a little over two hours later Shawn pulled back the curtain surrounding his hospital bed. He'd discouraged his brother from coming to the hospital, but he'd known the effort would be wasted breath.

Ryan scowled. "I told you not to come."

"The doctor has already discharged Nadia. Gideon is with her," Shawn said.

Ryan felt the tension in his body dissolve and with it the annoyance he felt at Shawn's presence. "I'm just waiting on my discharge papers."

Shawn sat in the metal chair next to the bed. "I got an update from the deputies. They found the car that hit you. A rental. Name on the contract is a fake, but the identification was good enough to fool the clerk."

The nurse had offered painkillers, but Ryan had refused. Now the headache swelling behind his eyes had him rethinking his decision. "None of this makes sense. How did they know where to find us?"

"You sure you weren't followed?"

Ryan hit his brother with a scorching look. "We weren't followed."

"Well, somebody knew you were heading to Rhode Island today."

He trusted the employees of West Security implicitly, but he knew that Nadia had informed Olivia and the general managers of the hotels that she wouldn't be in the office today. He hadn't thought it necessary to keep where they were heading a secret. A number of people knew they were headed for Rhode Island: Olivia, Erik and several employees at West Security for starters. He'd told Shawn they hadn't been followed, but he couldn't be sure. He mentally kicked himself for having let his guard down.

"Hey." Shawn clapped a hand on Ryan's shoulder. "Don't worry about it. We'll figure it out."

"I could have gotten Nadia killed."

"But you didn't." Shawn withdrew his hand, running it over his bald head before crossing his arms. "Look, I knew you had a thing for Nadia Shelton, but it seems like there's more to your feelings than you just being hot for her. I don't have to tell you how bad that can end. For you."

Shawn had been there for him the last time—the only time—he'd thrown professionalism aside and fallen for a woman he'd been paid to protect. The chemistry was off the charts, and he'd fallen for her hard. But when the danger faded, so had her feelings for him.

"I've got it under control."

Shawn let out a weary sigh. "You may be further

gone than I thought. Bro, Nadia is great. Smart, so-phisticated, and has a body that—"

Ryan growled a warning at his brother.

Shawn raised his hands in surrender. "What I'm trying to say is right now you're her knight in shining armor, Black Panther and 007 all rolled into one guy. But when this is all over, you'll still be a glorified bodyguard, and she'll still be the heiress to a hotel chain. Never the twain shall meet. You know what I'm saying?"

Ryan understood what Shawn was getting at. He even understood his brother meant to protect him, and he loved Shawn for it. He'd said the same thing to himself a thousand times in the last two days. Nadia was out of his league.

Unfortunately, a little voice inside his head told him it was too late. He already cared about Nadia too deeply. The only thing he could do now was ensure the only heart broken when this was all over was his.

"I hear you. I'm not too involved," Ryan said.

Shawn's expression made his disbelief clear.

Ryan wasn't in the mood to continue the conversation, however. "Was Eugene able to find anything on the security tapes from the Harlem hotel that might help us identify our arsonist?"

"He cleaned the tapes up pretty good. There's still no way to get a positive identification on the guy, but I got to thinking about you finding Andrei Ledebev's body so soon after the fire, which made me wonder if maybe it could have been him," Shawn said.

"And?"

Shawn shook his head. "No way. Wrong body type and coloring for either of the Ledebevs."

Ryan scrubbed his hands over his face. "The fire feels different from this other stuff that's happened. If we assume Nadia being pushed into the street was intentional—and I believe in my gut it's a part of this—then all the attacks except for the fire have been personal and physical. The fire seems aimed more toward the hotel itself."

"Yeah, but Nadia is the hotel in a sense. She owns it. She runs it. She keeps her office there. The hotel could be seen as an extension of her."

Ryan didn't disagree with Shawn's logic, but his gut was still telling him something was off about the fire. The doctor chose that moment to return with the discharge papers, so he and Shawn would have to wait until later to discuss the situation further.

Ryan listened to the doctor's admonishment to take it easy and rest, a suggestion he didn't bother to pretend he'd be following, and headed out to meet up with Gideon and Nadia.

Nadia's head popped up as he exited the sliding glass doors separating the exam area from the waiting room. She hurried to him, Gideon following in her wake.

"How are you?" she asked, placing a hand on his bicep.

Concern for him darkened her brown eyes, and his heart fluttered at the sight of it. He tried for a smile, but the deepening creases in her forehead suggested it had come out as more a grimace. "Just needed a few stitches, and I'm as good as new. How about you?"

"I may have a headache for a day or so. A couple ibuprofens will take care of it."

"You were both lucky," Shawn said. "Things could have been a lot worse. I'm guessing you still want to go to Rhode Island?"

Ryan nodded. He stole a glance at Nadia and found her doing the same.

"Okay. Northpath, here we come."

THE REMAINDER OF the drive to Rhode Island was, thankfully, uneventful. Nadia pretended to sleep for most of the trip. She understood the need for personal protection at the moment, but she desperately needed some time to process everything that had happened in the last couple of days. Ryan hadn't come right out and said it, but she got the feeling that things were going to get worse before they got better.

Nadia pretended to awake as Shawn pulled the car to a stop in front of a midsize hotel. A row of red-brick buildings with matching black awnings lined the cobblestone sidewalk as if they were the Queen's Guard. Antique lamp posts and the blue-purple sky cast shadows on those braving the chilly evening to spend cocktail hour outdoors.

Shawn returned from checking them in and announced he'd gotten them adjacent two-bedroom suites. They had just enough time for Shawn and Gideon to drop their bags in one of the suites before heading to the police station.

She'd overheard Ryan on the phone with Sheriff Charlotte Haley on the ride. The sheriff seemed understanding when Ryan explained that they'd been in a car accident. She'd been happy to push their meeting to six, meaning they now had a little over a half hour before they had to be at the sheriff's office.

The police hadn't allowed them to get their bags from the trunk of their totaled car. Shawn and Gideon offered to go to the big-box store outside of town to pick up basic toiletries and necessities while she and Ryan spoke with the sheriff. Since they were working with a single car, Shawn dropped Nadia and Ryan off in front of a sandstone building with imposing columns guarding the front entrance.

A deputy led them through a maze of desks and into Sheriff Charlotte Haley's spacious office.

"I'm glad you two made it in one piece." Sheriff Haley leaned back in her chair, her sharp eyes examining them.

Nadia sat beside Ryan on the other side of the sheriff's desk. A stout woman with red hair shot through with a generous dose of gray.

"We expected to be here hours ago. Unfortunately, as I said on the phone, we met with some trouble. Someone tried to run us off the road on the way here."

Ryan filled the sheriff in on the details of being forced off the road. As he spoke, Sheriff Haley's expression changed from one of alarm to concern.

"The driver didn't attempt to see if the crash killed you, though?" Haley asked when Ryan finished.

Lines formed on Ryan's forehead. "Not that we could tell."

"And no one approached you at the hospital, Miss Shelton?"

"No." Nadia looked from the sheriff to Ryan. They seemed to know something she didn't. "What am I missing?"

Sheriff Haley shot a look at Ryan.

"If the person who forced us off the road wanted to hurt you, they had the perfect opportunity to do so when we crashed," Ryan said.

"But they didn't take it," Nadia said.

"The crash could have been an attempt to separate you from your bodyguard here. That would make it a lot easier to kidnap you if that was the goal, especially in a busy hospital, but since no one approached you there…" Sheriff Haley shrugged.

"So what does that mean?" Nadia asked.

Ryan shifted awkwardly in his chair. The ER doctor had stitched his cut and prescribed a painkiller, which Ryan had declined to fill before leaving the hospital. Nadia knew he had to be in pain, but he hadn't complained once.

Neither Ryan nor the sheriff immediately answered her question. "Ryan?" she asked again.

"I don't know." Ryan shook his head. "But this incident feels different from the others. Whoever's doing this has been persistent from the start, so why did they walk away when we were in no position to fight back?"

"It is a conundrum, but you folks came up here to

ask about Miss Shelton's brother's accident," Sheriff Haley said.

"We don't want to take up too much of your time, Sheriff. I've already reviewed your official report of the accident that killed Nate Shelton. What I'd really like is to hear your take."

Sheriff Haley narrowed her eyes at Ryan. "I won't ask how you got your hands on a copy of my file."

It was a question Nadia wouldn't mind an answer to, but Ryan remained silent and expressionless.

Sheriff Haley huffed. "If you read it, you know the important stuff."

"That depends on what you define as important. You noted the brake lines seemed worn," Ryan said.

"Yes." Haley's tone was cautious.

"*Seemed worn.* Those were the exact words you used in the report. Not *were worn*," Ryan pressed.

Nadia's gaze flicked between the two of them. They were talking in code again. "Since I'm not fluent in whatever coded language you two are speaking in, would you mind saying the unspoken parts out loud, please?"

"What did you see that made you think Nate's accident might not be an accident, Sheriff?" Ryan asked bluntly.

Nadia gasped, her mouth falling open at the implication in Ryan's question.

Sheriff Haley seemed less surprised. "You're good."

The sheriff studied Ryan for a moment longer. "There was nothing I could prove, or you better believe I'd have chased it down to the end. I had an expert take a look at them, but the results were inconclusive. Still, the brake lines didn't look like any I'd ever seen worn. That doesn't mean it wasn't just regular wear and tear."

"But it got you thinking," Ryan pressed.

"Yeah. And when we couldn't find any reason for your brother to be in our little town…" Haley's voice trailed off, but she leaned forward, resting her arms on her desk, a questioning gaze focused on Nadia.

"I don't know why Nate was here. I assumed…" Even though he was gone, Nadia was hesitant to say anything casting Nate in a poor light. Her brother had his vices, but he was a good man.

She cleared her throat. "I assumed Nate came here with a woman. Those first days after Nate's death I was pretty out of it. Uncle Erik took care of all the paperwork and brought Nate's things back to New York."

"Erik Jackson. I interviewed him. He was quite torn up about your brother," Sheriff Haley said.

"Uncle Erik and Nate were close," Nadia replied. "Uncle Erik dodged all my questions about what Nate did in Northpath. I loved my brother, but I was well aware of his faults, including his penchant for dalliances with married women."

"Sheriff, there was something else in your report I wanted to ask you about," Ryan said, changing the subject. "You included a bunch of information about high and low tide and water flow in the sound. Why?"

"Well, you know our working theory was that Mr. Shelton's body was carried out to sea with the tide. It's possible, and hydrologists are expensive. In the absence of evidence of foul play, I couldn't justify spending the money for one." The sheriff's voice held more than a note of uncertainty.

Nadia's heart began galloping in her chest.

"But I've lived in this town all my life. I know the tide as well as I know the streets of this town. The tide that night was not strong enough to carry Mr. Shelton's body out to sea. I told your uncle all this when he was in town. I figured with your kind of money, you'd commission a hydrologist report."

Sheriff Haley tipped her head down, looking at Nadia over the top of her glasses. "To be honest, I expected to see you in my office months ago, Miss Shelton."

## Chapter Ten

Shawn and Gideon were waiting in the car in front of the sheriff's office when Nadia and Ryan exited. It didn't escape Nadia's notice that cars appeared to be a difficult space for her and Ryan to navigate. At least one of them seemed to be annoyed with the other every time they were in one together. That or someone was trying to kill them.

If Shawn or Gideon noticed the tension, they didn't comment on it during the ride back to the hotel. Nadia hadn't felt comfortable asking Shawn to pick up clothes for her, but he'd done so, anyway. A modest nightshirt, a peach cardigan set and a pair of jeans that miraculously looked like they might actually fit were in the bags on the back seat when she and Ryan got into the car. He'd even picked out a camisole and a three pack of cotton underwear, a purchase that saved her from having to wash out her undergarments in the bathroom sink. She made a mental note to write a check to Shawn to cover the cost of the clothes.

The four of them agreed to meet for dinner in fifteen minutes and each pair retreated into their suite.

Nadia carried her bag of new clothes into the larger bedroom, not caring that she'd commandeered the room.

"You're angry with me."

She turned to find Ryan standing, arms crossed, in the door to the bedroom.

"Why would you ever think that?" She ripped the tag from the cardigan with enough force to leave a small hole and silently swore.

He crossed the room, pulling a key chain from his pocket as he did, and held a small Swiss Army knife out to her.

"I wasn't sure the sheriff had suspicions about the accident. It was more a feeling than anything concrete."

She turned to face him, full-on ignoring the offer. "Then, why didn't you tell me what you were thinking?"

He exhaled heavily. Lifting her hand, he dropped the key chain in it and sat on the edge of the bed, looking up at her. "Because you are Nate's sister. You're emotionally involved in this on so many levels. I didn't want to throw out theories that might be hurtful to you without evidence."

"So you thought it would be better to just spring it on me in the sheriff's office?" She didn't try to hide the incredulity in her voice.

Nadia sat beside him massaging her temples. Another headache threatened, but she didn't think this one had anything to do with the bump on her head.

"Are you okay? Do you want another painkiller?" Ryan asked.

"I should be asking you that." She raised her gaze to his. "I just don't understand any of this. Are you saying you and Sheriff Haley think Nate's accident could have been intentional? Like murder?"

"It's possible."

Fear pounded in her chest, even as her head rejected the notion. Even with everything she'd been through, it was hard to imagine Nate having been involved in something that would get him murdered.

She studied Ryan. "But you don't think so. If not murder, then what?"

His forehead creased. "Why do you think your uncle didn't tell you about Sheriff Haley's theory concerning Nate's death?"

Nadia clenched her teeth, biting back her initial response to him dodging her question. If he thought she would forget about it, he had another think coming. But she was curious enough about his line of questioning to play along for a bit.

"My guess? Just like you, he thinks he needs to protect me from information that might stun my weak female sensibilities."

Her chest rose and fell in time with her accelerated breathing, not all of which could be attributed to the anger and frustration she felt. Even at her most annoyed, heat crackled between them. Their position, sitting on the large king-size bed, didn't help to quell the fire building inside her.

Ryan exhaled slowly, an obvious attempt to rein in his temper. "I never called you weak."

"You treat me like I'm weak. Maybe Uncle Erik is right. I should have been more involved in the investigation of Nate's death." Regret gnawed at her. "If there was something questionable about his accident, I owed it to him to find out."

Ryan took her hand in his and squeezed. "You were grieving. You can't blame yourself."

Easier said than done. She blamed herself, and she had every intention of making things right as soon as she returned to New York. Starting with hiring the hydrologist. But first, she had to make one thing clear to Ryan.

"Look, I know where I am, Ryan. I wouldn't be here, in this hotel room with you, in this situation at all, if Nate was a fine, upstanding, aboveboard businessman and nothing else," she said. "I don't want you keeping things from me."

Ryan held her gaze for several long moments. "I'm sorry. I'll keep you in the loop from now on."

Their gazes held for a moment longer before Ryan rose and walked to the door.

Nadia followed him into the living room of the suite. "To answer your question for real, Uncle Erik could have been trying to protect me, but he also might not have believed the sheriff's theory."

She watched Ryan take a bottle of water from the minifridge, waving him off when he offered her a bottle. "You've seen how resistant Uncle Erik is to the tiniest bit of criticism of Nate."

Ryan's brows scrunched together. "Has he always been that way about Nate?"

She sat on the large beige couch while Ryan leaned against the television console, his Adam's apple bobbing as he took a long sip from the water bottle, her mind going to thoughts of what it would be like to rain kisses along his neck.

"Nadia?"

She tore her gaze from his neck in time to catch his amused gaze.

"You okay?"

"Yes, sorry. Um…" She cleared the frog from her throat and rewound to the conversation they'd been having before she'd gotten distracted. "Uncle Erik and Nate have always been close, almost like Nate was a surrogate son to him. Their bond became even tighter after my father passed away."

She hoped Ryan didn't notice the tinge of jealousy in her voice. Her uncle had never slighted her, but he'd never attempted to get close with her either, not like he'd done with Nate. Maybe it was just because he related better to Nate as a male, but she couldn't say that it didn't bother her just a little.

"I think you should hire that hydrologist," Ryan said.

"I'd already planned to do it as soon we get back to New York. I don't even know where to start looking for one. I guess you can search for anything on the internet."

Ryan smiled. "West can probably help you with finding a reputable hydrologist."

"You don't trust the internet." Her smile was full of mirth.

"The internet can be a great place for finding all kinds of information about things and people. Good and bad." His tone turned serious. "But we need someone good who can work fast. I have a feeling all this is going to come to a head soon, and it seems we're behind the eight ball."

"What else should we be doing?"

Ryan's eyebrow rose. "We should not be doing anything. We aren't in this together, Nadia. It's my job to protect you and find out who is attacking you."

Irritation erupted in Nadia. "We just had this discussion, and you said you'd keep me in the loop."

"And I will, but I will not put you in danger. You'll know of any significant information we find, but I can't have you out here playing Nancy Drew."

"Nancy… You know what? This isn't going to work." She stood. "You're already going back on our agreement, treating me like the weak link again. If you can't handle me being a part of this, then I'll find an agency that can. You're fired."

Ryan also rose, his hazel eyes blazing. "You no longer want West to track down whoever is attacking you and provide your personal protection?"

Her hands found her hips. "That's what *you're fired* means."

"Fine." He closed the distance between them. "Then there's nothing stopping me from doing this."

He slid his hand around the back of her neck and brought his mouth within an inch of hers and stopped, waiting for her consent.

She didn't hesitate to close the remaining gap.

His mouth moved seductively over hers. It was a kiss that was both hungry and skillful. She reacquainted herself with the feel of his arms around her, sliding her arms up his chest and around his neck. She deepened their kiss, pulling him down into the couch cushions. His hand slipped under her shirt and up her torso to cup her breast, drawing a moan from deep within. She reached for the snap on his pants just as a knock sounded on the door.

"Ry? You in there? We going to dinner or what?" Shawn called from the hall.

Ryan drew back, his gaze a blaze of desire, his arms still locked around her.

"Hang on," Ryan called to his brother. "Am I still fired?" he asked Nadia.

His question hit her like a punch to the gut. She pulled from his arms. "Is that why you kissed me? To keep your job?"

"No, I…" He reached for her, but she took another step away. "Nadia."

"Ryan, what's going on in there?" Shawn called from the hall.

She held Ryan's gaze for a moment longer, unsure of what she saw in his eyes. Spinning, she went for the door to the suite, opening it to find Shawn's meaty fist raised for another knock.

"Everything okay?" Shawn's gaze flicked between her and Ryan.

"Fine." She forced her lips into a smile as she strode past Shawn and away from Ryan.

ALTHOUGH IT WAS the first time she'd ever been to Rhode Island, none of them were up for going any farther than the hotel restaurant for dinner. Ryan caught Gideon and Shawn up to speed on the information Sheriff Haley had relayed. Shawn lamented the fact that Nate's car had been destroyed. There was no way to have a look at the brake lines now, but he assured Nadia that he knew of a hydrologist that could help them. The foursome agreed to head back to New York at five the next morning.

Nadia's phone rang as she and Ryan entered their suite.

"Are you able to get New York news up there?" Olivia's harried voice carried through the phone.

"I don't know, but I'm sure I can stream it," Nadia said sitting on the couch and reaching for the laptop she'd left on the coffee table earlier. "Why?"

"There's a report on the fire at the hotel. The reporter is making it sound like a Shelton employee may have started it."

Nadia typed in the URL for the news station she regularly watched online. The station's website popped up almost immediately.

"*...the fire at Shelton's Harlem property was intentional. The NYPD would not comment, but* *sources tell WNYC News that police suspect it could have been an inside job."*

NADIA WATCHED AS her picture came on-screen.

"Sources say CEO Nadia Shelton abruptly left town the day after the fire. We have reached out to Miss Shelton for comment but have not been able to reach her."

Nadia paused the computer screen. "That reporter made it seem like I doused the room with gasoline and lit a match myself."

"What do you want me to do?" Olivia asked.

Nadia's stomach churned. She needed to squelch this rumor before it got out of hand. "Release a statement. The hotel is cooperating with the police investigation, and all Shelton properties are safe and open for business as usual."

"And if any of the guests ask questions?"

Nadia rubbed her temples. "Tell them that there was a small fire in an area that is closed off to the guests, and the hotel is one hundred percent safe. We're staying the night in Rhode Island, but I'll be in tomorrow morning."

"Great." Relief rolled palpably through Olivia's voice.

"And Olivia, thanks for holding down the fort while I deal with all this other stuff."

It didn't take much to imagine Olivia's ear-to-ear smile on the other end of the line. "No problem, boss."

Ryan had taken a seat next to her on the couch

while she watched the news stream and spoke with Olivia. She turned to face him now.

"I don't know how much more of this I can take." She tossed her cell on the coffee table beside her laptop. "I'd always dreamed of taking over Shelton with Nate. He was so good at being the face of the company. Dealing with the press and marketing and all that. I'm just not sure I can be the one standing in front of cameras convincing people that all is well. I'm not even convinced all is well."

Ryan took her hand. "You can, and you will. I've seen firsthand how hard you work and how much you love this company. You've had a lot of stuff thrown at you in a short period, but you're still standing."

She slid her hand from his. The only thing she knew for certain at the moment was that she wasn't thinking clearly, and his touch only compounded that problem.

"Maybe I should sell to Aurora. Mike was right about our margins being tight. If we get a reputation for being unsafe, guests will stop coming and events will stop booking with us. We can't survive that, not even for a little while."

"Have you considered that that might be the reason behind tonight's broadcast?"

She shook her head in confusion. "What do you mean?"

"Mike Dexter was in your office yesterday implying that it would be detrimental if news of the fire being intentionally started by an employee got out."

She gaped at Ryan for a minute while the picture he'd started painting solidified in her mind.

"That slimy… Tipping off the press would be just like him."

"The information West collected on him suggests he's a ruthless and not always ethical businessman. That said, we don't know for sure he was the source of the information."

"He's the source. When I get back to Manhattan I'm going to…"

She let the thought trail off. There wasn't anything she could do, at least not to Mike. He'd never admit he was the source, and whatever damage he'd intended to do to Shelton was already done. The only thing she could do was mitigate it by showing the world that she was in control and on top of things at Shelton. And that was just what she planned to do as soon as she got back to the hotel tomorrow.

Ryan had fallen silent as her mind drifted. She looked down, surprised to see he'd reclaimed her hand and started drawing small circles on her palm with his thumb. The action was at once soothing and exciting. Her mind flitted back to their earlier kiss, and heat swelled in her.

*Stop.*

The last thing she needed was another man jerking her around. So they were attracted to each other. That wasn't something either of them could control, but they didn't have to act on it. He'd made it clear on the ride up that he wanted to keep their relationship professional.

*And what about you? Do you want to keep things professional?*

She shook the thought from her head. It didn't matter what she wanted. He'd made himself clear, and he was right about her needing his help.

"About what I said earlier…" Nadia began.

"I didn't kiss you to keep the job," Ryan said.

She wanted to believe him. "Can we just forget about it? All of it?"

"Nadia—"

She held up a hand. "Please?"

He frowned but nodded.

"I should head to bed. We have an early start tomorrow." She rose and headed for the bedroom.

"Sure."

She could feel his gaze on her, but she kept her eyes focused on her bedroom door.

"Nadia." Ryan spoke as she turned the handle.

She threw her shoulders back and turned, meeting his gaze.

He stood in front of the couch, his gaze unreadable. "Good night."

## *Chapter Eleven*

Nadia waited until Shawn and Gideon joined them in their suite before coming out of her bedroom, foreclosing any chance Ryan might have had at discussing the events of the night before. Not that he had a clue what to say. Professional propriety, not to mention common sense, told him not to get involved with a client. He didn't want to make the same mistake twice. But his heart said something else entirely, and with each passing minute, he feared that he was already too far gone to change course now.

The drive back to New York the next morning was quiet but not uncomfortable. Ryan left Gideon and Shawn at West headquarters after Shawn assured Nadia he'd contact her soon with the name of the hydrologist. Ryan had promised to keep Nadia in the loop, and he intended to do so. But he wouldn't saddle her with the weight of more unproven theories. Getting a hydrologist to look at the water-flow patterns in the bay on the night of Nate's accident would go a long way in answering many of the questions about her brother's death. First and foremost, was Nate Shelton dead?

Ryan could understand Nadia's inability to see where the evidence pointed. Nate was her brother, and she loved and trusted him implicitly. But the absence of a body, the possible inability for the tide to have carried a body out to sea on the night of the accident and the fact that the brakes may have been tampered with were too many coincidences to ignore. Nate Shelton had the money to disappear and reinvent himself, and he knew people who could help him do it. The question was why? Why would a well-off businessman with familial ties chuck his entire life?

That was a question Ryan couldn't answer. Not yet.

After a quick stop at his place so they both could change before work, Ryan drove them to the hotel. He pulled the car to a stop in front of the Harlem hotel just after ten. The sliding door on the gray-paneled van parked three cars away slid open. A woman with a microphone in her hand bounded toward them as he opened the passenger door for Nadia.

"Miss Shelton? Alexandra Maloney, from WNYC News." A bearded cameraman trailed behind her.

Ryan positioned himself between Maloney and Nadia, but that didn't deter the reporter. "Care to comment on the fire at the hotel and the police investigation into whether someone working for you intentionally started it?" Maloney called out as they walked to the front of the hotel.

Nadia kept her head up but avoided looking at the reporter. Ryan kept one hand on her back, shepherding her into the hotel.

"I have sources that say the police are specifically looking at you, Miss Shelton."

The reporter's timing was terrible. Ryan had just opened the door to the hotel, and all eyes in the lobby turned to the scene occurring on the sidewalk.

He felt Nadia stiffen. She turned, taking a step away from the hotel's entrance toward Maloney.

"Your sources are mistaken, Ms. Maloney. There was a small fire in a guest room. It was quickly extinguished, and no guests were ever in any danger. There is minimal damage to the room and no damage to any surrounding rooms. The hotel is perfectly safe, as are all Shelton hotels. We are open for business as usual."

Nadia shot the reporter a smile that could freeze water before turning and marching into the hotel.

Olivia met them in the lobby and walked with them to Nadia's office. "You did well. You were cool, calm and collected, and you made the fire sound like no big deal. Just one of those things that happens sometimes."

"Right, just one of those things that happens right after someone breaks into my home and right before I find a body in my brother's apartment."

Olivia cast her eyes down at the files she held.

Nadia sighed. "I'm sorry. Being snarky isn't going to solve this."

"I think you've earned a bit of snark." Olivia smiled. "Anyway, it's rare I see you anything less than the consummate professional in the office. Gives me hope that you aren't as perfect as you seem."

Nadia returned Olivia's smile. "Not anywhere near perfect." She sighed. "Well, we need to get serious. The local news running a story about the fire is one thing, but if they get wind of the attacks on me and the note implying Nate is alive, we'll be pulled into a maelstrom."

"Did you find out anything helpful in Rhode Island?"

Ryan stepped into the reception area for Nadia's office, leaving Nadia to fill Olivia in on their trip to Rhode Island. He called Shawn, getting the name and contact information for the hydrologist, a professor at a college upstate. She was more than happy to look over the police report and other information and provide her opinion, especially after the fee Ryan quoted.

He'd just ended the call with the professor when Detective Parsmons entered the office suite.

"Detective, any news on the fire investigation?" Ryan asked.

Nadia and Olivia exited the office and joined Ryan and Parsmons.

"The fire inspector is leaning toward arson, but it's not official yet. You probably know as well as I do that the camera footage was grainy and unhelpful. But I'm not here about the fire."

"No? Well, what brings you here, Detective?" Nadia asked.

Parsmons tipped his head in Ryan's direction. "I'm here to place Ryan West under arrest for assault."

A thin chuckle burst from Nadia, her eyes darting between the two men. "This must be a joke."

Ryan kept his eyes glued to Parsmons. The set of Parsmons's jaw left no doubt that his words were no joke.

"Who am I accused of assaulting?" he asked, even though he was sure he already knew the answer.

"Michael Dexter. You have the right to remain silent…"

He didn't listen to the rest of the Miranda warning. He didn't need to. He'd have liked to say this was the first time he'd been arrested, but that was far from the case.

"I'll hold off handcuffing you until we get outside in deference to Miss Shelton."

Nadia, who seemed to have been in a trance since Parsmons started reciting the Miranda warning, came alive. "This isn't right. Mike assaulted me. Ryan was just defending me."

Parsmons's eyes narrowed. "That's not how Mr. Dexter tells it. In any case, he filed assault charges, so my hands are tied."

"I'll be okay," Ryan said. "Call Shawn and tell him what's happened, please."

He wasn't even sure Nadia heard him.

Nadia's nostrils flared as she faced off with Parsmons. "Your hands may be tied, Detective Parsmons, but mine aren't."

NADIA MET SHAWN and another West brother, Brandon, at the police station. Brandon noted that having eschewed the security business in favor of the law had come in handy on multiple occasions. A few hours after he'd been arrested, Ryan had been arraigned and released on minimal bail.

Shawn gave them a ride back to Ryan's apartment and helped them carry in their bags before leaving them.

Nadia helped Ryan lower himself slowly onto the sofa, a groan slipping from his lips.

"How are you feeling? Should I get you a pain-killer?"

"No, I'm fine."

"I can't believe Mike filed charges against you," Nadia called over her shoulder as she walked into the kitchen. She filled a glass with water and crossed back to Ryan. "I'm so sorry. You're in this mess because of me."

Ryan took the glass. "Don't apologize to me. I shouldn't have lost my temper. I embarrassed him, and guys like him lash out whatever way they can when they're embarrassed." He took a drink.

"Well, I won't let Mike get away with this."

He reached for her hand, pulling her down beside him. "Let's not discuss this right now."

She sat beside him and let her head fall to his shoulder. He reached his arm around her and pulled her closer. They'd discussed keeping things on a professional level just yesterday, but right now she didn't care. Life seemed to be lobbing hand grenades at her at every turn, and she needed to feel his warmth and ensure he knew she was there for him. And if they were truly being honest with themselves, they'd passed professional days ago. She was practically living with him, for goodness' sake. You couldn't get more unprofessional than that.

"You must be tired. You should go rest." Ryan ran his hand along her arm.

She laid her hand on his hard chest and felt the beat of his heart. She should be tired, but exhaustion was the furthest thing from her mind. Hyperaware of him next to her, arousal swept through her body.

"I'm not sure I can," she said.

"None of this is your fault," he replied, misunderstanding her comment.

"No, but in the last two days you've been hospitalized and arrested, all because you're helping me."

He pulled her closer. "You can't think like that. We'll figure this out soon. I promise."

"It's hard to think at all right now. Not when all I want to do is this."

She ran her hand over his stubbled jaw and covered his mouth with hers.

Heat crackled between them. She wanted more than just kisses. More than just making out like crazed sixteen-year-olds in his parents' basement. She wanted him, and his body hardening against her right now proved he wanted her just as much.

Ryan pulled away, but the lust in his eyes was clear.

"I want you. I know you're attracted to me." She wasn't usually this forward with a man, but she was tired of holding back.

"Of course, I am, but I don't want you to regret anything. Right now your emotions are heightened because of the situation, but when it's over, I'll still be a glorified security guard and you'll still be a hotel heiress."

"I've wanted you for six quarters."

"What?"

"Our first quarterly meeting about hotel security was six quarters ago. I knew I wanted you that first day. This drama I'm embroiled with now has only made me see how short life is and that I should go for what I want."

"And what do you want?"

"You."

She couldn't remember ever feeling more vulnerable. For a brief moment, she thought he'd pull away again. Then his hand curled around the back of her neck, and his mouth closed over hers.

The spicy scent of his cologne mingled with the minty taste of his mouth, igniting a passion inside her she'd never experienced before. She wanted to touch every inch of him. She threw one leg over his body, straddling him.

She wasn't usually the aggressor when it came to sex, but she wanted to leave no doubt in Ryan's mind that she wanted to be with him in this way, at this moment.

She tore at the buttons on his shirt, her mouth never leaving his. He met her urgent fumbling with equal desperation, dragging her shirt over her head.

*There'll be time for a slower exploration later.*

That this was just the first time of many they'd be together excited her even more. When he closed his mouth over one hard nipple, his hand skimming under the lace edges of her panties, she moaned her encouragement.

"You are so perfect." He trailed kisses across her chest, lavishing her second breast with the same attention he'd paid to the first. "You don't know how many nights I've dreamed of doing this. Of touching you. Making love to you."

"As many nights as I've dreamed of being with you."

He slid a finger inside her, and she lost the ability to say anything further. Lost the ability to think about anything other than wanting him inside of her.

She drew him into a long, deep kiss that sent them both into overdrive.

She rose to chuck off her jeans and underwear, and he did the same, pulling protection from his wallet before letting his pants fall to the floor. She took the condom from him, rolling it over his arousal slowly before straddling him again.

He took her face between his hands. "Are you sure?"

She lowered herself in answer, taking him inside, bearing down until he was completely within her.

He moaned, bringing a smile to her face. She rotated, and he grasped her hips, thrusting upward. She set the pace, slowing things down with long, slow movements. He skimmed his lips over her neck, to her jaw and back, sending her arousal soaring. Her back arched with the pleasure, and he used the opportunity to capture a nipple between his teeth, stroking it with his tongue.

"Ryan," she cried out as raging hot need exploded within her. She moved her hips faster, frantically racing toward the release they both craved.

Ryan pulled her closer, even as his thrusts grew more hurried, uncontrollable. He claimed her mouth as they climaxed together.

They stayed locked that way for several minutes, coming down from their explosive lovemaking. It wasn't until she finally rolled away that she remembered the gash on his side.

"Oh, I forgot about your injury. I didn't hurt you, did I?" She ran her hand over his bandage.

He caught her hand, brought it to his lips and kissed her palm. "Baby, nothing about what we just did hurt."

She felt her cheeks heat.

Ryan pulled her back into his side but angled them so they could look at each other. "Are you okay?"

She knew what he really asked. Did she regret what they'd done?

She pressed her body closer to his, her bare breasts pressing against his chest. His arousal swelled, and she fought the desire to touch him.

"I am so much better than okay." She smiled a flirty smile. "Want me to show you?"

His smile was laced with desire. "How about I show you a thing or two," he said, rising over her and forcing her to lie back on the couch.

She laughed, then lay back and enjoyed the show.

## Chapter Twelve

Nadia awoke with a start. It took her a moment to place where she was. Ryan's bedroom. They'd retreated to his bed after ordering in dinner from the Chinese restaurant on the corner. They made love twice more, exploring each other more fully each time before falling into a sated sleep. But he wasn't in bed beside her now.

Shadows danced over the room. She wasn't sure what had awoken her, but a creak from outside the bedroom set her heart pounding. Something was very wrong.

A shadow moved at the side of the bed. A hand came down over her mouth before she could scream.

Her eyes adjusted to the darkness in the room, and Ryan's face came into focus hovering over the bed.

"Shh. Roll off the bed, and stay down."

She did as he said, her heart thumping in her chest. She wedged herself into the space between the bed and night table.

Ryan rose and put his back to the wall. She caught a flash of silver in his hand. A gun.

She barely had time to process what was happening before the door to the bedroom swung open slowly.

Ryan raised his gun. "Freeze."

The figure at the door swung toward Ryan, his gun outstretched.

Two pops sounded in quick succession.

She did scream this time, unable to stop the sound from bursting from her throat.

The man at the door swore. His gun clattered to the floor, and his right hand flew to his left shoulder. He ran from the room.

Ryan sprinted for the bedroom door. "Don't move."

She didn't know if she could move even if she'd wanted to. Fear paralyzed her.

A crash sounded from the other room.

She couldn't stay cowering in the corner. Ryan could need help.

Nadia eyed the gun the intruder had dropped. She didn't know the first thing about guns—she'd never even touched one before the previous day—but she couldn't leave Ryan to fend for himself. She grabbed the gun from the floor and raced from the room.

Ryan and the intruder grappled in the living room. The intruder landed a punch to Ryan's stomach, sending him doubling over. The man grabbed the Guggenheim book from the table next to the sofa and swung it at Ryan, catching him on the side of the head. Ryan fell onto the sofa, stunned.

"Stop!" She pointed the gun at the intruder.

Blue eyes held her in a sinister gaze. The man took a step in her direction.

She kept the gun outstretched, but the quiver in her hands increased to a tremor.

The intruder paused, his gaze traveling to her shaky hands. That he questioned the wisdom of attempting to take the gun from her was written all over his face.

Ryan pushed up from the sofa, and the intruder turned, dashing toward the apartment entrance. He was out the door before Ryan made it onto steady feet.

Ryan's eyes landed on her. "Are you okay?"

"I think so. Yes."

Ryan stepped next to her, wrapping his steady hands around hers and taking the gun from her. He set it on a nearby table and guided her to the sofa. "Sit. I've got to secure the apartment and call the cops."

She grasped Ryan's arm before he could walk away. "Why is this happening?"

His eyes flashed in anger, but his touch was gentle as he ran his thumb over her cheek. "I don't know, honey. But I promise you, I will find out and make it stop."

DETECTIVE PARSMONS WAS not happy that Nadia and Ryan were involved in yet another *incident*, as he referred to it. He'd declared Ryan's apartment a crime scene.

They were quickly running out of places to stay, but Ryan ensconced them in one of West Security's safe houses about an hour outside the city.

Numb from exhaustion, Nadia barely made it through her nighttime routine before falling into bed.

Morning came sooner than she'd have liked. Ryan tried to talk her into taking the day off. Hanging around the safe house wondering what would happen next held no appeal, and as long as Ryan was by her side there didn't seem to be any reason to avoid going to work.

Ryan kept a go bag in his car for himself, but they headed to Nadia's apartment so she could change before heading to the hotel.

Just as before, Gideon met them at the apartment, but this time Shawn was with him. Gideon again stood guard in the hall while Shawn stayed in the lobby keeping an eye out for trouble. Nadia had no idea what her neighbors thought about the cadre of big scary men traipsing through the building the last several days, but since they were New Yorkers it may not have raised any eyebrows at all.

Ryan followed Nadia into the apartment, but he remained just outside her bedroom when she went in to change. Taking a breath, she yelled through the door, "It's obvious the guy that broke into your apartment last night is connected to the dead guy we found in Nate's apartment."

She grabbed her favorite blush-red suit, tossing it on her bed before diving back into her closet for the black silk blouse she always wore with it. Her power suit, she thought, because she never lacked for confidence when she rocked it.

They'd kept the conversation light and to a minimum on the drive into the city from the safe house. But with the closed door between them, she felt more comfortable broaching the subject.

"I think that's a safe bet," Ryan answered.

She pulled the blouse over her head before speaking again. "Since all the other attacks were clearly aimed at me, it's also safe to assume that the guy last night was coming after me too."

The thought of what could have happened if Ryan hadn't been there sent a shiver down her spine.

Wiggling the skirt over her hips, she zipped it in the front before spinning it around her hips.

"Also a safe bet."

She could hear the tension in Ryan's tone.

She grabbed her black kitten heels and suit jacket.

"So how did he know I was at your place?" Nadia said, pulling the door open simultaneously.

Ryan leaned against the door frame, his arms crossed over his chest, his biceps bulging.

She pulled up short, just inches from smacking into his hard body.

He didn't flinch. Ryan had several inches on her. His head dipped in a slow, appreciative gaze that heated every inch of her as it passed over her body.

"I like the suit," he said, his voice husky.

Nadia wasn't sure she could breathe, much less speak. After a too-long moment, she swallowed hard and forced words from her throat. "Thank you."

Ryan's mouth turned up in a sexy smile, and he took a step back.

Nadia slid past him, her eyes cast down at her feet.

She made it to the couch and sat, putting on her shoes.

"To answer your question, it wouldn't have been that hard to figure out you were staying at my place."

It took a moment for her to remember she'd asked a question.

"If they've monitored your apartment, they know you aren't staying there. And I've been sticking to you like…" Ryan's eyes flashed with an emotion she couldn't name but that sent a zing of excitement through her. "Well, I've been staying close. I never thought anyone would be stupid or reckless enough to breach my home. These guys are more desperate than I thought."

"Desperate isn't good, is it?" Nadia stood, donning her suit jacket.

"No, it isn't. Which is why I don't want to stay here any longer than necessary." Ryan grabbed the handle of the bag she'd packed before changing and led her to the door.

Having completed their duty, Gideon and Shawn headed back to West's headquarters while Ryan drove Nadia to the hotel. It was after ten when they arrived, and although check-out wasn't for another hour and Olivia was helping the clerk, there was a line at the reception desk.

Nadia hurried through the lobby to the door leading to her offices, Ryan on her heels.

As a boutique chain, they didn't have the same hiring luxury as larger hotel chains. Calvin Shelton had been adamant that employees of his hotels knew how to do more than one job, and it was a rule that applied doubly to his kids. Pitching in as a desk clerk for a few hours was just part of the job, even for the CEO.

Nadia unlocked the door to her office, intending to drop her briefcase and purse on her desk before heading back out.

The man sitting behind her desk brought that plan to a sudden halt.

In one swift motion, Ryan shifted Nadia behind him and reached for the gun under his shirt.

"I'd rather you not." The man nodded toward the door Nadia and Ryan had just entered through, and they turned.

A second man, almost as wide as the door frame, stood gun in hand.

"I would just like a few moments of Miss Shelton's valuable time. Of course, I expect you want to stay, Mr. West. Please have a seat," the man directed with an authoritarian benevolence.

They sat in the chairs facing her desk.

"Do you know who I am?" the man asked.

Ryan answered, "The authorities haven't been able to get many pictures, but I'm guessing you are Lincoln Smith."

Smith bowed his head. "A pleasure to meet you both."

Ryan seemed to know who Lincoln Smith was, but the man in front of her was a complete stranger to Nadia.

"I apologize, but your name doesn't ring any bells for me."

Smith looked surprised that she'd spoken. Nadia

speared Smith with a cool stare, despite his menacing demeanor. He was in her office, sitting behind her desk, and if he thought she would play the silent woman in this drama, he could think again.

Smith's smile was slick as oil and just as cold. "It's always humbling to realize one is not as well-known as one believes. You may not know me, but I believe you have met my associate, Mr. Brian Leroy."

Nadia frowned. "I have."

"I found it unfortunate that Mr. Leroy's company was not awarded the contract for the work on your last hotel." The iciness in his tone had her tensing. Ryan also tensed.

Smith raised a hand. "It is what it is, in this business. One can't expect to get every contract." But his tone made it clear that is exactly what he would have liked.

"In any case, your brother made a much more interesting business proposition." Smith pinned Nadia with his stare. "One which I took him up on."

Nadia's brain clouded with confusion. "I don't understand. What business proposition?"

Smith cocked his head. "It's best you know as little about that as possible. But you can be of help to me. I need to know where your brother is."

Anger and frustration broke through the other emotions coursing through her. "Serenity Valley Cemetery."

Ryan sent her a cautioning look, which she ignored.

Smith's eyes darkened. "I'm not a man to be played with."

"Neither am I," Ryan intoned.

Smith's attention swung from Nadia to Ryan.

She felt the man standing behind her shift.

The tension in the room cut through her anger. "I assume you are responsible for the note asking about Nate, as well as all the other incidents that have happened to me and my hotel in the last few days?"

Smith's forehead wrinkled. "I don't know what happened at your hotel. I directed a few employees to locate your brother. They used you to draw him out."

"Nadia has nothing to do with your business with Nate Shelton." Ryan glared at Smith.

Smith shrugged. "They are contractors. I don't question their methods as long as they do the job."

Ryan shot daggers at Smith.

"Fortunately for you, you are very resourceful, Miss Shelton." Smith shot a glance at Ryan. "And my men very inept." Smith frowned. "I'd hoped a few warnings—the calls, the damage to your car— would scare you enough that you'd reach out to your brother, giving my men a chance to locate him. However, whoever attacked Mr. West's home yesterday in an attempt to get retribution for Andrei Ledebev was not authorized or condoned by me."

Nadia glanced at Ryan. "We had nothing to do with that man's death."

Smith waved away her comment. "It's of no concern to me if you were. Hazards of the job. Taras is bereft over the death of his brother and acted rashly. I will deal with him."

Another jolt of fear ran through Nadia's body. She didn't want to know what Smith intended.

"An internet search would have given you my brother's location. He died almost a year ago."

Smith locked on to Nadia's face. After a long moment, the hostility in his eyes morphed into disbelief. "You really don't know?"

Nadia looked at Ryan, wondering if he understood what Smith was saying, because she certainly didn't.

Ryan reached for her hands, which she clutched so tightly in her lap her knuckles had gone white.

Smith motioned to the man standing behind them. The man stepped around the desk, pulling a letter-size envelope from the inside breast pocket of his jacket.

Smith handed a five-by-seven photograph across the desk.

Ryan and Nadia both scooted forward in their chairs, Ryan's hand still covering hers.

The picture showed a man with a shaved head and full beard but still recognizable as Nate.

Nadia's heart shuddered, an audible gasp slipping from her lips. "It's Nate."

Ryan squeezed her hand. "That does not prove Nate's alive."

"The date-time stamp," Smith said simply.

The picture had a date and time stamp in the bottom right corner. It had been snapped a month ago.

"Time stamps can be faked," Ryan said.

Smith spread his hands in front of him in a gesture of innocence. "What reason would I have to falsify the photo?"

Ryan didn't have a good answer for that question, but he knew enough not to trust Smith.

"It can't be," Nadia whispered, despite everything in her screaming that it was Nate. Nate was alive a month ago. If what Smith said was the truth, Nate was alive at this very moment.

"I'm sorry." Smith's eyes held sympathy. "I figured you knew. My men almost had him, but…well, I obviously need to improve my hiring practices."

Smith looked away for a moment, seemingly lost in thought. When his gaze returned to Nadia, any trace of sympathy was gone. "However much of a shock this is to you, the fact remains that your brother stole from me."

Smith's words were a second punch to her gut. "What? How?"

"As I said before, it's best you not know the details. Since it is obvious you know nothing about my business with your brother or his deception, I will leave you out of this, as long as you produce Nathan within forty-eight hours."

That didn't sound at all like he was leaving her out of it, but she didn't have time to say so.

"And if she doesn't produce Nate?" Ryan scowled at Smith.

Smith's gaze dropped the temperature in the room ten degrees.

"I'm sure neither of you want to find out the answer to that question."

# Chapter Thirteen

Smith left the same way he'd appeared to have arrived, without being captured by the supposedly upgraded security in the hotel.

Ryan made a mental note to order a full review of the hotel's security and find out how Smith had gotten in. He called Dale, the West Security member stationed in the hotel lobby, the moment Smith stepped foot out of Nadia's office.

Dale arrived in Nadia's office ten minutes later. He'd done a sweep of the lobby and exterior of the hotel but there was no sign of Smith. Dale explained that a guest had approached him and reported seeing a strange man entering her room as she'd gotten off the elevator. Given the circumstances, he'd gone to check out the room and, finding it empty, had proceeded to the security room to check the tapes for the man. That's where he'd been when Ryan called.

Ryan sent Dale back to the control room to pull the video showing how Smith got into Nadia's office. Even having distracted Dale, Smith would have needed a key card to access the area. This was the second time someone had accessed an area of the hotel with a key they shouldn't have had, and Ryan wanted to close this security loophole ASAP.

"I can't believe Nate is alive." They were the first words Nadia had spoken since Smith had left.

"If he is. We can't just trust Smith. This could be some kind of trick."

As soon as he could, he'd have the technology whizzes at West examine the photograph to determine if it was genuine.

"He is. That picture." Nadia pointed to the picture that Smith had left behind. "It's Nate. And when I saw it I knew. How could he do this?"

If Nate really had stolen from Smith, he had a very good reason to want to disappear. Smith may not be the boss. Still, he had to pay the bosses just like all the other midlevel mobsters, and when it came to getting their cut, they wouldn't care that Smith had been ripped off. In fact, if the bosses found out Nate had stolen from him, it would have made Smith's position within the organization precarious. Smith had several reasons, personal, financial and political, to want to make an example out of Nate. Or someone close to Nate.

A vise closed round his heart.

Ryan pushed down the rising fear. It wouldn't help him keep Nadia safe, and that was the only goal at the moment. The best way to keep her safe was to find Nate.

He called Gideon and Shawn and relayed the conversation with Smith. After a copious amount of swearing, Gideon got started on a deep search of Nate's and Nadia's lives to turn up any leads on where Nate might be.

No matter how motivated, it was difficult to disappear completely. Humans are creatures of habit with a deeply rooted instinct to gravitate toward things, areas and people familiar to them on some level. Even if he'd moved to a new city and assumed a new name and career, it was likely that Nate still listened to the same music and frequented the same kind of restaurants. Those were all threads West Security could follow to find him. Of course, they usually had more than two days to pull those threads.

"Do you have a scanner? I want to get those pictures to my tech guy. Maybe we can see some detail that will tell us where they were taken."

Nadia showed him the machine, and he made quick work of scanning the pictures and sending them. He mentally kicked himself for not asking Smith where the photographs had been taken. Hopefully, they could get something helpful from the photos.

While he spoke to Eugene Paul, he kept an eye on Nadia. She stared quietly across the room, lost in thought.

Ryan ended the call.

"The listings." Nadia looked at him with glassy unfocused eyes.

"What?"

"Smith said Nate and he were involved in a business deal. And Nate had those listings for the buildings for sale in the Bronx."

"You think Nate and Smith's business deal involved buying those buildings?" Ryan turned the possibility around in his head. "It's a place to start, but I'm not sure I remember the addresses, and Parsmons hasn't released Nate's apartment yet."

"One was 1437 Ambrose Avenue." Nadia rose and moved behind her desk. She logged in and typed the address into the search bar.

The listing popped up on-screen.

She reached for the phone on her desk. "I'm going to call the realtor. See what information I can get about the property."

Ryan skimmed the listing. It gave the name Carol Alvarez as the realtor.

Miss Alvarez picked up on the second ring.

"My name is Nadia Shelton. I'm interested in one of the properties you have for sale. 1437 Ambrose Avenue."

"Are you representing a buyer?" Through the speaker, Alvarez's voice dripped with suspicion.

"No, I'm not a realtor." A sucking sound came from the other end of the line. Ryan imagined Alvarez readying to end the call. Nadia spoke quickly. "I'm the CEO of Shelton Hotels. I'm always looking for opportunities, and this property came to my attention."

"It's a great property." Enthusiasm laced Alverez's tone now. "A lot of potential. The entire block is for sale."

Ryan searched Alvarez's brokerage website for any properties for sale on the same street. Listings for four adjacent properties appeared.

"Although the properties are listed separately, the sellers have a strong preference for selling the buildings together. I realize you may not be interested in all four," Alvarez blurted, obviously anticipating that most buyers are not in the market to purchase an entire city block. "But there was another potential buyer not long ago, and they may be interested in forming a partnership with an interested party such as yourself."

"Another buyer?" Nadia asked.

"Yes, the buyer had an exclusive option to purchase the properties last year. Unfortunately, they weren't able to get financing."

"Do you mind me asking how much the buyer paid for the option?"

"Ten million." Nadia turned to Ryan, her eyes wide.

He motioned for her to keep talking.

"Yes, well, and what is the seller asking for the combined properties?"

"One hundred ten million."

Under different circumstances, Nadia's stunned expression might have been comical.

"Miss Shelton? Are you still there?"

"Yes, I'm here. Well, we are in the beginning stages of scouting properties. I'll be in touch if I decide to pursue one or more of the properties."

"Of course." Alvarez's palpable disappointment carried over the phone line.

Nadia moved to replace the receiver, then stopped. "Miss Alvarez?"

"Yes?" The other woman's voice rang over the line hopefully.

"Would you mind telling me the name of the buyer who had the option?"

Alvarez hesitated.

"If I am going to consider a partnership, I'd like to know who I'd be working with," Nadia added, glancing at Ryan.

"I guess it wouldn't hurt. It was an LLC. Abebe Holdings."

Nadia's back stiffened.

"Do you have the name of a contact person for the LLC?"

Sounds of paper shuffling came from the other side of the line. "Here it is. Erik Jackson."

RYAN DIDN'T TRY to talk Nadia out of going with him to confront Erik with the information Carol Alvarez had given them. Without knowing exactly how deep in this mess Erik was, it would have been safer for Ryan to speak with Erik alone, but he understood Nadia's need to confront the man she trusted.

Having Nadia along also made it easier to get past the security in the lobby of the law firm. The guard on duty merely sent Nadia a cheery smile and waved them both through the gate.

They took the elevator to the forty-second floor.

Nadia had said very little since they'd left her office. Now she almost radiated with anger.

Nadia stepped from the elevator before the doors had completely opened and stormed down the brightly lit corridor toward an office at the far corner. An older lady with a gray bob sat at a cubicle off to the side of the door. She looked up from her computer screen, her welcoming expression changing to one of surprise as Nadia blew past, flinging the door open hard enough that it slammed into the wall.

Ryan caught it before it bounced back, but Nadia was already across the large office, stopping in front of her uncle's desk, her hands fisted on her hips.

"Where is Nate? I know he's alive. I know he was involved in some business deal with Lincoln Smith that went wrong."

Erik hurriedly replaced the phone receiver he'd been speaking into and rose. "Nadia, you need to calm down. I don't know what you think you know."

Ryan's eyes narrowed in on the butterfly bandage covering Erik's right cheek and the brace on his left wrist. He caught Erik's gaze, and the guilt swimming in the man's eyes was unmistakable.

"I know," Nadia yelled. "I spoke to the realtor, Carol Alvarez. I know about the buildings in the Bronx, Abebe Holdings and the ten-million-dollar option. You're listed as the contact person on the documents, Uncle Erik."

Ryan laid a hand on Nadia's shoulder, concerned she might launch herself over her uncle's desk and physically attack him.

Not that Erik looked like he would put up much of a fight. He visibly shrank with each word from Nadia's mouth. Erik fell back into his chair.

There was a long moment's pause. "How did you find out?"

"Does it matter?" Nadia answered incredulously.

Anger boiled in Ryan's stomach. Erik didn't seem to grasp the seriousness of the situation. "Lincoln Smith dropped by Nadia's office this morning for an impromptu meeting."

Erik's face went ashen.

Maybe he was coming to understand the danger his and Nate's lie had put Nadia in. Lincoln Smith was a killer, and he'd been within feet of Nadia. If that didn't make this situation real for Erik, nothing would.

"He showed me pictures of Nate. Pictures taken a month ago. Why, Uncle Erik? Why did you and Nate do this?" Nadia's voice cracked.

Ryan's heart pinched. Nadia didn't deserve to be put in this situation by the people she trusted the most.

Erik sighed heavily. "We didn't have any other choice. Nate wanted to make a name for himself, outside of what Calvin had built. He saw this project as a way to do that. You can't understand a man's need to prove himself to the world." Erik straightened in his chair.

Nadia felt anger flare in her gut. "Lots of people, men *and women*, want to prove themselves, Uncle Erik. They don't throw in with the mob, though."

Erik's gaze dropped to his desk. "I don't know if Nate realized who he was doing business with, not at first. His friend Brian Leroy brought him the deal initially."

Ryan resisted the urge to call Erik a liar. They had most of the story, but Ryan had no doubt that Erik either knew where Nate was or how to get in contact with him. Since they needed that information, he reined in his temper.

"By the time Nate came to realize his partner wasn't the businessman he'd thought, it was too late. And then the financing fell through, and things spiraled."

Nadia sank into the visitor's chair in the office. Ryan stood behind her. "How did Nate get ten million dollars to buy the option?"

Erik sighed. "Smith put up the money for the option, with Nate acting as the front man due to Smith's reputation. Nate was supposed to come up with half the hundred-ten-million-dollar purchase price, and Smith would supply the other half."

"Fifty-five million? How did Nate expect to raise that?" Nadia asked, her voice rising.

Erik leaned forward, locking gazes with Nadia. "You have to know Nate was adamant about not using any of Shelton Hotels' assets for this deal. He wanted to do it all himself."

Ryan pressed his lips together. That Erik would justify his nephew's stupid decision to get involved with mobsters, even after everything that had happened, boggled the mind. But he and Nadia still needed Erik to tell them where Nate was, so Ryan would keep his mouth shut, for now.

"You think I should, what, give him a prize for that?" Nadia said.

Erik's eyes turned hard.

Ryan interjected before the man could respond. "Could we get back to my question? How did Nate plan to raise the twenty million?"

"Nate is a Shelton. He has friends. Connections. Only, it was more difficult than he could have expected. The option was about to expire, and he didn't have anywhere near what he needed.

"And Smith would lose ten million dollars. A loss like that was not something Smith and the people he answered to would just write off."

"So Nate faked his death and went into hiding." Ryan cut to the end of the story.

Erik nodded. "Nate figured if he died in an everyday car accident, Smith wouldn't have cause to be suspicious." Erik shrugged. "Car accidents happen every day."

"But Smith didn't buy it?" Ryan said.

"It seemed like he had. But then Nadia told me about the men at her apartment and the fire at the hotel. Even then I wasn't sure if any of this had to do with Smith until..." Erik's voice trailed off.

Ryan could guess where this part of the story was headed.

"Until what?" Nadia looked from her uncle to Ryan, confusion clouding her eyes.

"Until Andrei Ledebev showed up at Nate's apartment while your uncle was there," Ryan answered for Erik. It was a shot in the dark, but it made sense that Erik could have been staying over at the apartment on the night Andrei broke in.

Erik's gaze pleaded. "It was self-defense. He attacked me. I had no choice."

Nate's apartment was probably one of the worst places for Erik to have used for his overnight stays in New York under the circumstances. As soon as Smith realized Nate was alive, he'd have scoured the city real-estate records for other properties in Nadia's or Erik's name looking for Nate.

Nadia covered her mouth with her hand, the color fading from her face.

He hoped she wasn't about to be sick. He needed her to hold on for a little while longer. Then he'd get her somewhere safe and bring Nate in. After that, he wasn't sure what would happen. The best thing for Nadia would be if he turned Nate over to Smith, but Ryan was sure Nadia would object, and it would sign the man's death warrant. No matter what Nate had done, Ryan wouldn't aid cold-blooded murder. But first things first.

Ryan locked eyes with Erik. "Where's Nate?"

The older man looked ready to argue for a moment before all the fight seemed to be expelled right out of him like air from a balloon.

"I don't know." Erik's gaze listed left.

Nadia surged to her feet. "Enough lies, Uncle Erik," she said, slamming her hand on his desk. Ryan rose to stand beside her.

Erik started, his chair rolling away from his desk. "I don't know for sure. But he calls me weekly, just so I know he's okay."

"What's the number?"

Erik shook his head. "It's always a different number."

"So you never call him?" Ryan asked.

"I've called him a few times. Always on the last number he used to call me. Sometimes it works, sometimes it doesn't. I called Nate yesterday to tell him about the note Nadia received at her office asking about him."

"Give me the number you used to call him." Ryan took a pen from a holder and tossed it on the desk in front of the man.

Erik puckered his lips but picked up his phone, scrolled for a moment, then scribbled a number on a sticky note.

"What else can you tell us?" Ryan asked.

"Nothing." Erik held up his hands. "Nate has to be careful. I get the feeling he moves around a lot. The phone numbers he calls from usually have different area codes."

That meant very little these days, with easily acquired burner phones and numbers, but he didn't mention that to Erik.

"Nate's never said anything about his location?" Nadia asked.

Erik hesitated.

"Uncle Erik, Smith knows Nate is alive. The only

chance he has is if we find him and he goes to the police."

"I really don't know where Nate is. Not for sure. But a while back he complained about his boss. Some disagreement, I can't remember over what, but it doesn't matter. His boss shut him down and said something like 'It's the way it's always been done at the Delaney, and it's the way it always will be done'."

Nadia gripped Ryan's arm. "The Delaney Hotel? In Atlanta?" Her voice rose in excitement.

Erik looked as if he'd aged a decade since they'd walked into his office. "I don't know. I don't even know if he referred to a hotel, but that's what I assumed."

Ryan pulled up the website for the Delaney Hotel on his phone. "It's a place to start. One more thing before we leave. How did you get those injuries?"

Erik hesitated. "I was in a car accident."

Erik didn't meet Ryan's eyes when he spoke, but Ryan didn't let his gaze leave the man's face. He was already sure he knew the answer, but he wanted to see the older man's reaction to the question. "It won't be difficult to find out where you were yesterday."

Silence hung in the room for several long minutes.

"Uncle Erik?"

Erik raised his head, his eyes watering as he looked at his niece. "I just wanted to keep you from going to Northpath."

Nadia gasped and reached for Ryan. "You forced us off the road."

"When you left that message saying you were

going to Northpath to talk to the sheriff, I panicked. The sheriff was suspicious from the beginning. I couldn't let her put those ideas in your head."

Tears rolled down Nadia's cheeks as she stood up. She speared her uncle with a look of contempt before turning her back to him and starting for the door.

Ryan followed suit.

"You may not believe this," Erik called out, "but your brother and I love you. We did this to protect you."

Nadia turned back to her uncle. "No, he didn't. His ego got him into this mess, and now his cowardice could get me killed."

Nadia didn't wait for her uncle's response before striding from the room.

Ryan followed, unclenching his fists. He would have liked to have had a private chat with Erik, but he didn't have the time to make the man understand how foolish it was to have tried to fake Nate's death. Or how deeply he and Nate had hurt Nadia in doing so.

"I need to head to my office to put together a game plan for bringing Nate back to New York," Ryan said once they were back in the car.

Nadia nodded. "Whatever you think is best."

"I'm glad you said that, because I think you should stay here while I go to Atlanta."

Nadia shook her head. "I told you I didn't want to be left out."

"I'm not leaving you out. But we don't know what we're walking into. We can't call Nate and tell him we're coming. He's bound to be on edge since he's on the run. It's too dangerous to take you."

She pushed her shoulders back. "I. Am. Going. With you."

He shook his head, his jaw clenching.

"Nate won't know you're coming. Who knows how he'll react? If I'm there, he'll know you aren't working for Smith."

He could see her point, but his every instinct told him she should stay in New York.

"Nate's safety isn't my primary concern. Yours is."

Nadia's gaze was unreadable. "I'm concerned about Nate's safety."

After everything her brother had put her through, she still put him before herself. It was why he loved her.

*He loved her.*

Despite all the reasons he shouldn't, didn't even want to, he did.

"Please." Nadia's voice broke through his thoughts.

They still had most of the forty-eight hours Smith had given them to find Nate. But they couldn't be sure Nate was still in Atlanta or if he had even truly been there in the first place. Flying down there could end up being wasted time, but they had nothing else to go on.

Ryan navigated them through city traffic. "Okay. But you do what I say. I'm not taking any chances with your safety."

Nadia reached over the console between them and took his free hand. "Thank you."

While he drove them to the safe house, she called Olivia to let her know that they wouldn't be back to the hotel today.

When they arrived, he ran his usual check of the premises, making sure the windows and doors were locked. Then he did what he'd been aching to do since they'd left Erik Jackson's office. He pulled Nadia into his arms.

She stiffened for a millisecond before sliding her arms around his waist and burying her face in his neck. They stood that way for several minutes, her hot tears soaking his collar before Nadia stepped back out of his arms.

"I'm sorry." A rueful laugh slipped from her lips. "I've been pushed into oncoming traffic, chased by madmen and shot at all within a week, and then I fall apart when I get good news. Nate's alive. I should be ecstatic."

He kissed her forehead before placing a light kiss on her lips. "You've had a lot thrown at you. It will take some time to process it all. Until then, you feel how you feel."

"I'm going to lie down." She turned away, but stopped and turned back before disappearing down the hall. "When will we leave for Atlanta?"

"I've got to coordinate some things with Shawn, but this evening."

She nodded. "I'll be ready." Nadia headed to the bedroom before facing him again. "Thank you."

The bedroom door clicked shut.

He didn't want to go chasing after Nate. He

wanted to wrap Nadia in his arms and spirit her away from all this madness for good.

That wasn't an option right now, but soon. He'd do his best to get her brother out of the mess he'd gotten himself into, but getting Nate back to New York was only one piece of the puzzle. Getting him clear of Smith would be infinitely harder.

And when this was all over and Nadia was safe, he'd tell her how he felt. Because he knew now that this wasn't just a passing infatuation spurred by the intensity of their situation.

It was the real deal.

## Chapter Fourteen

Ryan tried the number Erik gave him for Nate, but the call went directly to voice mail. Nate Shelton wasn't a stupid man. Even burners had GPS nowadays so their users could use mapping and directional apps. That meant that the phones could be tracked, even though it was much more difficult to track burners than standard phones since they weren't associated with contracted carriers. Lucky for them, West Security did the impossible every day.

He made reservations for them at the Delaney. They'd probably get there too late to talk to many of the staff, but he'd booked a suite for two nights so they'd have a legitimate reason to be at the hotel all day tomorrow. Given the time crunch, he hoped they wouldn't need to stay the second night.

Ryan let Nadia sleep for as long as he could, waking her when there was a little more than an hour to get to the airport. She'd showered, packed and was ready to go fifty minutes later. He drove them to a private airstrip in the Bronx.

A dark blue sky hung overhead as he drove into

the airport, though the tarmac was amply lit. Nadia's eyes grew wide as Ryan pulled to a stop beside a sleek white jet idling in front of one of the hangars, its steps already lowered.

They got out of the car and moved to the trunk.

Nadia looked from the plane to Ryan. "Does every security firm have a private jet on standby?"

He smiled, lifting his bag onto his shoulder. "The plane is a loan. A while back we rescued a wealthy client's son from a group of kidnappers. The client was appreciative and offered his plane if we ever needed it."

"You called in a favor for me?"

If he counted the IOUs he owed his brothers, he'd already traded several favors helping her find Nate. He'd call in a hundred more if it would keep her safe, but now wasn't the time to get into that. He simply answered "Yes."

Nadia touched his arm, sending a tingle through him. "Thank you."

His eyes locked on hers, and despite the time and place, the urge to tell her how he felt overwhelmed him. "Nadia, I'd do—"

"Mr. West?" A thin woman in a dark blue suit, white shirt and practical pumps approached from the hangar. "We're ready to board you and your guest now."

The woman made a sweeping gesture toward the plane, her practiced smile fixed in place.

He held Nadia's gaze for several seconds then

swung her bag from the trunk and followed her to the plane.

It wasn't the first time West Security had borrowed a plane from this particular client, but since the client owned at least three private jets that Ryan knew of, he wasn't surprised to realize he'd never flown on this plane before. Custom cherry woodwork and beige leather seats as soft as butter greeted them along with the flight attendant. Traveling the world by private plane was a life many people dreamed of having. Ryan thought back to the crisis that had brought his client to West Security. The maxim *Be careful what you wish for* sprang to mind.

He and Nadia settled in, and the pilot had them in the air quickly.

Once they reached their cruising altitude and the attendant deemed it safe, he tried calling the number that Erik had given them for Nate again. The call went straight to voice mail, and Ryan hung up without leaving a message.

He leaned his head back on the seat, intending to take a moment or two to just relax. He awoke with a start as the plane bounced along a patch of turbulence. A glance at his watch told him he'd slept for nearly an hour and a half. He'd intended to work for most of the three-hour flight, but he'd obviously needed the sleep more.

Ryan looked across the aisle to where Nadia sat on the leather couch across from his seat, looking out of the window at the passing clouds.

"You're awake." She turned to him, a half smile on her face.

"Yeah. Sorry about that."

"Don't be sorry. You must be exhausted."

"I'd planned to work on the flight, but I did research the Delaney Hotel before we left. Given your industry experience, you could probably tell me more about the place than I learned, though. It's an icon, according to the internet."

Nadia's half smile turned full. "It is. It was built in the 1920s—I can't remember the exact year—and for a long time, if you were somebody and visiting Atlanta, you stayed at the Delaney."

"And now?"

"Times changed. The family that owned it sold, and the brand lost its luster. And then the Great Depression hit." Nadia shrugged.

"But the hotel survived."

"It did. One of the big international chains eventually purchased it."

Ryan raised a brow. "Aurora?"

His heart buoyed at her laugh. "Mike wishes." She named one of the other well-known hotel chains.

"I'm sure you'll find the building fascinating with your background in art. It's on the historic register, and the brand's been repositioned to appeal to guests who'll pay a premium for the architecture and historic charm."

*A premium* was an understatement. The room he'd booked had not been cheap.

"You know, we can't be sure that Nate is still

at the Delaney or if he ever was. Uncle Erik could have heard him wrong, or it could be another hotel named Delaney."

Ryan studied her. He saw a woman conflicted. She wanted to find Nate, but finding him wouldn't solve her problems. In some ways, it made them even worse. Smith had forced her into a position where she had to choose her brother's safety or her own. Could she do to Nate what he'd, however unintentionally, done to her? If it came down to it, could she sacrifice Nate to save herself?

"We don't, but it makes some sense that Nate would start over in Atlanta," Ryan said. "There's a family tie, even if he can't reach out to the family, and he's somewhat familiar with the city from your childhood trips. It's also a big enough city that he can blend right in. And with his knowledge of the hospitality industry, it makes sense he'd get a job at a hotel."

Nadia didn't look convinced.

He unbuckled his seat belt and moved to the couch where Nadia sat. "Hey." He took her hand in his. "We'll check in, get a good night's sleep and hit the ground running. Who knows, by this time tomorrow we could be back in New York with Nate."

Nadia's eyes locked with his. "Then what?"

He didn't have an answer for that, at least not one she'd want to hear. He pulled her close, and she laid her head on his shoulder.

"I don't know if I've said it before, but thank you." She didn't lift her head as she spoke. "I don't think I could have made it through all this without you and Shawn and West helping me."

He dropped a kiss on the top of her head. "You're the strongest woman I've ever met. You'd have done fine if you'd had to go it alone, but you should know that you never have to. I'll always be here for you."

They sat that way, with Nadia's head on his shoulder and his arms around her, until they landed.

IT WAS LATE by the time they arrived and checked in at the Delaney. Ryan had booked a suite, but this one didn't have two separate bedrooms like the suite in Richmond. Not wanting to be presumptuous or place any pressure on Nadia, he'd intended to bunk on the couch. Not that he'd planned to get much sleep at all. He wanted to do more research before morning and maybe take a tour of the hotel to see if he couldn't find a staff member or two willing to talk to him.

But by the time he and Nadia had eaten their room-service dinner, they were both exhausted. Nadia quickly disabused him of the notion of sleeping on the couch, and they fell into bed, wrapped around each other.

A beam of sunlight shot through the space between the closed curtains and illuminated Nadia's sleeping form. Her soft body snug against his, loose curls falling across his hard chest. Touching her creamy skin set his blood racing to his groin. Another morning, when they had more time and were free of the mess Nate had created, he'd make good on the thoughts running through his head. For now, he had work to do.

He rose from the bed and quietly made his way into the common area of the suite.

If Nate was in Atlanta, Ryan wanted to find him fast. He could almost hear the forty-eight-hour deadline ticking away like a detonator counting down the seconds before an explosion. Smith didn't issue idle threats. If they didn't turn over Nate, the dynamics of the situation would take a drastic turn for the worse.

He opened his laptop and scoured the background report on Nate for clues to help them figure out where he might be. He also researched the Delaney Hotel and its employees, giving thanks for the public penchant for oversharing on social media.

Water ran in the bathroom on the other side of the bedroom's door, calling his attention to the time. He'd spent the last hour and twenty minutes researching and had gotten a good start, although no concrete leads on Nate's whereabouts.

He called down to room service, hanging up the phone just as the bedroom door opened.

"I ordered breakfast."

"Great," she said, lingering near the bedroom as if she wasn't sure whether she wanted to come out into the living area.

"If you're done with the bathroom, I'll get washed up before the food gets here." Ryan strode toward the bedroom. There was only one bathroom in the suite, and it was through the bedroom door.

"Oh, yes, sorry." She moved into the living room and took a seat on the couch.

He ran through his morning routine, quickly showering, shaving and putting on fresh clothes. He reentered the living room just as Nadia closed the door to the suite.

A rolling table covered with a white tablecloth sat in the middle of the room with silver plate covers over the food and the morning paper perched at its edge. Nadia had moved the vase of flowers that decorated the round dining table in the room to the credenza behind the couch and set the table for breakfast.

"I should have waited until after the food arrived to shower," he said, pushing away the irritation he felt with himself. "I don't want you opening the door to anyone. We can't be sure who's on the other side."

Nadia froze with the plate cover she'd just lifted in her hand. "You think we could be in danger here?"

He took the cover from her, putting it aside and removing the covers from the other three plates on the tray. "I think I'm not taking any chances with your safety, so please don't open the door without me, okay?"

She nodded and sat, her expression pensive.

They ate in silence for several minutes.

"You know way more about how hotels run than I do. If Nate works or worked here, what kind of job would he have?" Ryan asked.

Nadia swallowed the piece of toast she'd been chewing. "Well, he's qualified for almost any job.

Remember I told you my father made sure we could do just about every possible job at a hotel. But I'm assuming he couldn't produce references, at least not good enough ones for managerial positions since he can't use his real name—"

"A safe assumption."

"Then, entry-level positions. Clerk, housekeeping, janitorial."

"He'd probably want to stay behind the scenes as much as possible," Ryan added. At least that's what he'd do if he was on the run. No telling who could walk up to check-in and recognize the clerk behind the desk as Nathan Shelton. Better not to take that chance, even if he was hundreds of miles away from Manhattan.

"Um…then janitorial, laundry or maintenance would be the most likely. Also, if the hotel runs the restaurant in the lobby, he might try for a kitchen job like dishwasher."

"Okay, then we'll target staff from those departments," Ryan said as he finished his omelet.

Nadia had eaten very little, mostly pushing pieces of egg around on her plate. "That's not going to be easy. The nature of those jobs has them behind the scenes."

Ryan stood. "We'll play it by ear. First, though, I want to walk around the hotel. Get the lay of the land."

They each grabbed a key and headed out the door.

The articles he'd read describing the Delaney hadn't done it justice. Much of the first floor had been given over to retail establishments, including four restaurants of varying cuisines. The lobby soared four stories and boasted cut glass skylights he hadn't noticed checking in after dark last night. They walked the hotel for nearly an hour, eventually finding their way to the lower level where half a dozen large conference rooms and twice as many smaller meeting rooms were situated. None of the rooms appeared to be occupied at the moment. Two oversize white doors showcasing the words *Staff Only Beyond This Point* stenciled in bold red font stood out among the sea of yellow on the walls.

"Laundry, janitorial services, housekeeping—pretty much the business end of the hotel—are probably behind those doors," Nadia said, heading for the doors.

"Hang on." Ryan grabbed her arm. "Let's just wait for a bit. See what we see."

She gave him a curious look but let him lead her to a sitting area at the other end of the hall where they could still monitor the staff door.

Hotel employees in black polyester skirts and pants with matching vests came and went through the staff door.

After ten minutes, Nadia slid to the edge of her seat, her hands twisting in her lap. "What are we waiting for?"

"If we're right that Nate would prefer a job that's out of sight, he'd most likely befriend similar workers. The people going in and out of this door aren't dishwashers, launderers or janitors—not dressed like that."

"You're right. There's probably a service hall and elevator on the other side of the doors. They'd use that to get around as much as possible."

He studied the doors. "Then, we're not going to find the people we want to talk to here."

Nadia snapped her fingers. "How about the employees' entrance? I should have thought of that sooner." Nadia glanced at the watch on her arm. "It's not quite nine. We could still catch someone coming in."

"It's worth a shot." Ryan stood, offering Nadia his hand. He pulled her to her feet. They took the elevator to the lobby level and exited the hotel through the main doors.

The hotel spanned the entire city block, but halfway along the length of the building, a service alley cut the building in two. A gray steel door with an assortment of dings opened into the alley. A black square keypad was mounted next to the door.

Ryan nodded toward the coffee shop across the street. "Let's have a cup of coffee."

Nadia squinted at him. "We just had a cup of coffee."

Ryan took her hand, pulling her across the street. "Let's have another."

He bought their coffee and steered them to a table on the outdoor patio that gave an unobstructed view of the alley and the door. The day was already starting to heat up, so they weren't the only patrons choosing to take their refreshments on the patio.

Nadia followed Ryan's gaze. "Ah, I see. More watching."

Ryan shot her an amused glance. "A lot of a private investigator's work is sitting and watching."

She laughed. "I'd be horrible at that."

They didn't have to watch long before the steel door opened. An employee clad in white trousers and a long-sleeved white shirt stepped into the alley and lit a cigarette.

"Bingo." Ryan rose, leaving his coffee on the table.

He and Nadia crossed back to the hotel side of the street. They skirted around a row of dumpsters emitting a vaguely noxious odor despite the closed covers.

The man blew a ring of smoke into the air and watched as Nadia and Ryan approached. "You're not supposed to be back here." The nameplate pinned to the man's chest read *Brian*.

Ryan smiled. "We'll only be a minute. We'd like to ask you a couple of questions."

Brian blew another ring of smoke. "What questions?"

"We're looking for someone who might work here or have worked here in the last couple months."

Brian threw his cigarette on the ground and snubbed it out with the toe of a scuffed red Adidas sneaker. "I don't want to get involved."

"Please." Ryan frowned when Nadia stepped in

front of him toward Brian. "I'm trying to find my brother. He's in trouble, and I just want to help."

Brian's eyes roamed Nadia's body from head to toe, lingering on her breasts. Ryan cleared his throat and fixed the man with a warning glare.

Brian's eyes snapped to Ryan's, a guilty smile twisting his lips.

"Please," Nadia said, drawing the man's attention back to her. "If you could just look at this picture and tell me if he works here?" Nadia held her phone out.

Brian sighed. He studied the picture on Nadia's phone for several seconds. "It looks like it could be Jamal. His head was shaved, and he had one of them skinny beards right here." Brian tapped the cleft in his chin. "But yeah, I think it's Jamal. He don't work here no more."

The familiar rush flowed through Ryan; the surge of adrenaline that hit whenever he was on the right track in a case.

"What's Jamal's last name?"

Brian tilted his head back, eyes turned to the sky in thought. "Fredricks, I think."

"Do you know where Jamal works now?" Ryan asked.

"Nah, man. He left, like, four, five months ago. We weren't friends or nothing. I just knew him from around."

"Was Jamal friends with anyone in particular?" Nadia followed up.

Brian hesitated, obviously reluctant to share the names of his coworkers.

"We won't say how we got the name," Nadia said.

Brian hesitated for a moment longer, then shrugged. "I guess it don't matter since I didn't give you my name, anyway. Jamal hooked up with one of the girls in housekeeping. Karen Vernon. I don't think she's on the schedule to work today."

His excitement waned. They didn't have a lot of time for tracking down people. Hopefully, there weren't a lot of Karen Vernons in Atlanta.

"Thanks, man." Ryan offered his hand, a twenty discreetly palmed.

Brian grasped Ryan's hand, taking the twenty without blinking an eye. He swiped a plastic square over the black box on the wall. The locks clicked open, and he pulled the door open.

Ryan and Nadia turned.

"Hey," Brian called before they'd taken more than five steps.

They turned back, Ryan angling himself in front of Nadia.

"I think she lives with her mother out in Myers Grove." Brian went inside without waiting for a response.

Nadia glanced at Ryan. "To Myers Grove?"

"To Myers Grove."

## Chapter Fifteen

Myers Grove was a working-class neighborhood approximately thirty minutes outside of the city. The homes were small and neatly kept. Ryan had called Shawn on the drive and had him run a basic check on Karen Vernon. He'd also passed on the fake name Nate had been using in Atlanta.

Thirty-two years old, Karen had worked at the hotel for the past seven years, rising to the rank of assistant manager of housekeeping services. With one ex-husband and no run-ins with the law, Karen was the model of an upstanding citizen.

Ryan knocked on the door of the white clapboard house Karen shared with her mother and ten-year-old son.

A woman in her midthirties with shoulder-length chestnut hair opened the main door but left the screen door firmly shut. "Can I help you?"

"Ms. Vernon? My name is Ryan West. I'm a private investigator, and this is Nadia Shelton. We'd like to ask you a few questions about Jamal Fredricks."

Karen took a step back, her eyes clouded with suspicion. "Why are you asking about Jamal?"

"I'm his sister. I need to find him. It's very important." Nadia took a step forward, assuming control of the conversation. Ryan let her. He'd interviewed enough people to know when one was close to slamming the door in his face. If tapping into the woman's sentimental side would help them get answers faster, it was worth taking a back seat.

"I can't help you. I'm sorry." Karen took another step back and began to close the door.

"Please. The man you know as Jamal is my brother, Nathan Shelton. He's in trouble."

Karen tilted her head and studied Nadia for several moments. "You look like him." She sighed and unlocked the screen door, pushing it open.

Ryan and Nadia stepped into the living room. The space was compact but tidy. Karen waved Nadia and Ryan to the couch, where they waited while she made coffee.

Karen returned with a tray holding three mugs. She set the tray on an ottoman and passed a cup to Nadia then Ryan before settling in the easy chair opposite them with her cup.

"You don't seem surprised to learn that the man you knew as Jamal is not who he said he was." Ryan started the conversation with the obvious observation.

Karen sighed. "I guess you already know Jamal and I dated for a while or you wouldn't be here." Karen placed her mug back on the tray and lowered her fingers. "The minute we met, Jamal—Nate and I connected. My mother thought we were moving too fast, but sometimes the attraction, not just physical stuff but something deeper, it just hits you."

Ryan caught Nadia's eye. A current of electricity sizzled between them.

Karen's gaze bounced from Ryan to Nadia, her mouth turned up in a half smile. "So you two do know what I mean." Karen's smile fell. "A few weeks after we started seeing each other, Jamal told me the truth about who he was and why he was in Atlanta."

"And you stayed with him?" Nadia said with surprise.

"Everyone makes mistakes and deserves a second chance." Karen shrugged. "And we love each other."

Ryan set his coffee aside and pushed to the edge of the sofa. "Do you know where Nate is now?"

Karen's eyes drifted up and to the left. "No."

"It's important we find Nate as soon as possible. The men he told you about know he's alive," Ryan said.

Concern coursed across Karen's face. "He thought someone was watching him, following him. That's why he left Atlanta."

"When was this?" Ryan asked.

"About a month ago."

That matched up with the dates on the photographs Smith had given them. Nate's instincts had probably saved his life, but his luck wouldn't hold out forever.

"Please, if you know where Nate is, tell us so we can help him," Nadia implored.

Karen sighed. "I don't know for sure. He calls at least once a week, but he's careful not to give any specifics. We use burner phones."

He read between the lines. "You don't know for sure, but you have an idea where he is."

Karen sighed again. "I drove him to the bus station and purchased his ticket for him. The bus lines only ask for identification when you purchase the ticket."

"So even if someone got a passenger list his name wouldn't appear." Ryan was glad to see that Nate wasn't completely oblivious about how to fly under the radar. Hopefully, it would be enough to keep him safe until they could get to him.

"Where was the ticket to?" Nadia asked.

"DC."

Another big city where the addition of one more person wouldn't be noticed by many.

Ryan rose and pulled out his phone to call Shawn and get him started on tracking down any Jamal Fredrickses in DC or the surrounding areas. They couldn't be sure he was still using the name Jamal, as doing so would be a huge risk, but good fake identification was expensive. Since Nate wasn't sure he was being followed, he might have considered it worth the risk. They couldn't even be sure he'd taken the bus all the way to DC, but it was a place to start.

The hum of adrenaline he'd felt after talking to Brian earlier had risen to a drumbeat. They were getting close to finding Nate. Their luck just needed to hold for a little longer.

THEY THANKED KAREN for her help and promised to let her know when they found Nate. Ryan drove them back to the Delaney while Nadia thought about what Karen had said. Had her brother really been in love? It seemed impossible that her confirmed bachelor of a brother had found love in the midst of the chaos that was his current life, but stranger things had happened. That he'd told Karen the truth about who he was and what he'd done went a long way to showing that maybe he had found love. She just hoped they could figure out a way for him to live long enough to enjoy it.

Ryan's phone rang as they entered the hotel lobby. "Shawn, what's up?"

He pulled Nadia into an alcove off the busy lobby and held the phone so they could both hear.

"No Jamal Fredricks in DC, but I checked the next biggest city on the bus route, Richmond, Virginia, and found three. Only one recently applied for a Virginia driver's license, though," Shawn said.

"I'm not even going to ask how you got that information so fast," Ryan replied.

"I'll shoot you what I have and keep digging. Are you guys going to head to Richmond?" Shawn asked.

Nadia glanced at her watch. It was still early in the afternoon, and Richmond was only an hour and a half flight.

"Yes. I'll let you know if that changes." He ended the call and turned to Nadia.

"So we're headed to Richmond now."

Ryan nodded. "I'm going to call the pilot now,

and then I'll let the front desk know we won't need the room another night."

"Okay. I think I'll head upstairs and start packing."

"Make sure to lock the door, and don't open it for anyone," he reminded her.

"Got it."

She took the elevator to their room, her mind on packing and the possibility that they'd find Nate before the end of the day. She didn't notice the movement from behind her until she'd already inserted her key card.

The locks on the door beeped open at the same time a large palm landed between her shoulder blades and shoved her forward.

She stumbled into the room, landing on one knee hard enough to make her teeth chatter.

It took a moment before she was able to push from the floor and turn to face her attacker.

When she did, she looked into the face of Taras Ledebev, the man who'd attacked her and Ryan in Ryan's apartment.

"Where's your boyfriend?"

"He'll be here any minute, so I'd run now if I was you."

Taras sneered. "Not running, girlie. I'm going to pay you and your boyfriend back for killing my brother."

Nadia glanced around the suite looking for a weapon within reach. Their breakfast dishes had been removed while they'd been out, dashing any hope of using a knife in self-defense. The only things within arm's reach were the newspaper that had been delivered with their breakfast and the vase of yellow roses, both of which were on the credenza behind the couch.

"We had nothing to do with your brother's death." She hoped keeping him talking would give her time to come up with an idea.

"He just happened to die in your brother's apartment," Taras growled. "I'm not that stupid."

"You're plenty stupid if you think I killed your brother. Or that you can get away with killing me and Ryan in a hotel full of people."

Someone pounded on the door. "Room service," a voice boomed from the hall.

Taras turned.

The door burst open, and Ryan barreled into the room. He rammed his shoulder into Taras's stomach. The two men crashed into the armoire. Ryan threw a punch, catching Taras in the jaw, momentarily stunning him.

Taras pulled a switchblade from his pocket. The blade snapped out.

Taras stepped forward, slashing out with the knife and missing before the two men tumbled to the ground. Taras straddled Ryan's legs and swung the knife down toward Ryan's face. Ryan rolled to his side, throwing Taras off-kilter. But not for long. Taras raised the knife again. Ryan gripped Taras's wrist with both hands, the two men struggling for control.

She couldn't just stand there and watch Ryan get stabbed.

Nadia grabbed the glass vase behind the couch. She rushed toward the struggling men and brought the vase down on the top of Taras's head.

Taras rolled off of Ryan, dazed but conscious, and ran for the door. He sprinted into the hall as Ryan pushed up from the floor.

"Stay here," Ryan called out as he followed Taras from the room.

Nadia stayed on the couch and rubbed her sore knee, coming down from the adrenaline high of the moments before.

Ryan was back in less than five minutes, but it seemed eons longer as she waited and wondered if Taras has gotten the jump on him again.

"He got away." Ryan locked the door to the suite.

"Should we call the police?"

Ryan hesitated. The police would ask a lot of questions he didn't want to answer at the moment. Reporting the intrusion would also eat up time they didn't have. "Let's report it to the hotel management as a simple break-in. Since nothing was taken, they'll probably be happy to go along when we decline to make a police report. I'll let Parsmons know when we get back to New York."

Nadia crossed to where Ryan stood, a slight limp in her gait.

"You're hurt." He slid his arm around her waist.

"It's nothing. I can walk it off. How did Taras

know we were in Atlanta?" Nadia asked more to herself than him.

Lines formed in Ryan's forehead. "He must have followed us to the airport in New York. I didn't see anyone tailing us, but that doesn't mean no one did."

"What now?"

"I'll call the front desk, and you pack. We have a plane to catch."

It took the hotel management nearly two hours to take their statements and document the damage to the room, but they were more than happy to handle the situation in-house. The plane was fueled and ready to fly by the time Nadia and Ryan arrived at the small private airport where they'd landed the night before. Thankfully, the flight from Atlanta to Richmond was short, but it was still late afternoon by the time they arrived.

Ryan gave his name at the check-in counter at the chain hotel where he'd had Shawn make them reservations.

The clerk punched several keys on the computer in front of him.

"Mr. West, welcome." The clerk beamed. "Your room is ready, and your companions have already checked in."

"Companions?"

The clerk's smile dimmed but held. "Yes. Mr. Shawn West and another gentleman. Mr. West asked me to tell you he is in room 4123 just a couple doors down from you."

Ryan barely stopped long enough to drop their

bags off in their suite before he hustled them to Shawn's room.

Shawn opened the door with a grin.

"What are you doing here?" Ryan frowned across the threshold at his brother.

"Hello to you too. You want to come in so you can lay into me out of earshot of the whole hotel?"

Shawn stepped back, opening the door to the room wider.

Nadia smiled as she walked past him into the room. "Hi, Shawn. Hi, Gideon."

Gideon nodded from his seat at the table in the hotel room.

Shawn strode back to the table and sat, leaving Ryan to close the door to the suite. "So what are you two doing here?"

Shawn's brows lowered. "Helping you. I got an address for Jamal Fredricks. A PI I've worked with before is there now with eyes on the place. He hasn't spotted Nate, but if he's got a job, he may not be home yet," Shawn said.

"What's this?" Nadia asked, pointing to the map spread out on the table in front of Gideon and Shawn.

"An aerial map of Nate's neighborhood," Shawn answered.

"Good." Ryan's tone was grudging. "We're on a tight timeline, but I want to know as much as possible about what we are going into. If Nate is smart, he's got himself some protection. I don't want any of our guys getting shot trying to bring him home."

"Nate wouldn't have a gun," Nadia said, drawing

the men's attention to her. Their parents had kept a close eye on them, but both she and Nate had lost friends to the epidemic of gun violence plaguing New York in the 1980s and '90s. "He hates guns." A tremor slivered through her at the memory of holding a gun on the intruder in Ryan's apartment. "We both do."

Shawn met her gaze. "People do things they'd never think of doing when they're in the kind of trouble your brother is in."

Shawn's statement hung in the air for a long moment. Nadia glared, but Shawn held her gaze, seemingly unaffected.

"Let's focus here." Ryan sat at the table next to Gideon, while Shawn went back to studying the map of Nate's neighborhood and planning how to approach Nate.

Nadia joined the three men but held her tongue as Ryan, Shawn and Gideon talked through possible scenarios for getting Nate to return to the city, from Nate willingly coming back with them to the need to remove him forcibly. She didn't like the idea of physically making Nate return to New York. It wasn't lost on her that some of the plan Bs they discussed technically amounted to kidnapping her brother, but there didn't seem to be much else she could do if Nate wouldn't come willingly.

*And then what?*

"What happens once we get Nate back to New York?"

Getting Nate back to New York wouldn't end this

nightmare. They'd still have to deal with Smith, and she wasn't about to just hand Nate over like a lamb to slaughter.

*One gigantic problem at a time.*

Ryan shared a look with the men at the table.

"The safest thing for you would be for us to turn him over to Smith," Gideon said emotionlessly.

Nadia pushed her palms against the table. "No."

"The alternatives?" Ryan said, sending Gideon a look that would have made other men shrink.

Gideon's expression didn't change. "We can try to work out a deal with Smith that ensures your and Nate's safety. Or go to the cops and set up a sting."

"I don't see Smith being willing to negotiate, not that we could trust his word, anyway," Shawn said. "But Nate has made him look bad, not to mention cost him millions of dollars. Smith needs to make an example of him."

"Okay, so we take option two." Nadia speared Ryan with a look.

"Going to the cops won't be easy either." Ryan shook his head. "Parsmons isn't sold on all the incidents being connected, and we haven't exactly kept him in the loop. We'd lose a lot of time just bringing him up to date and getting him on board."

"Not to mention completely lose control of the situation after we bring in the cops," Shawn chimed in.

"The NYPD can't mount an operation like this as fast as we can, and there's the little matter of them leaking like that strainer to the press." Gideon studied the documents on the table. "I've got a friend at the FBI's New York office. I've worked with her before, and I'm sure I could convince her to let us in on the op."

Gideon looked up when his statement was met with silence. "What?"

"I'm shocked to hear you refer to someone as a friend," Ryan teased.

"I'm shocked his friend is a woman. The perpetual scowling and grunting usually scares them off," Shawn said.

Nadia concentrated on the map on the table so Gideon couldn't see her smile. Despite the serious nature of the conversation, it was nice to have a moment of levity.

Gideon didn't appear to share her sentiment. His scowl deepened. "Do you want me to call her or not?"

"Yes," Nadia answered quickly before Ryan or Shawn could say something that might jeopardize her best chance for getting Nate out of this mess safely. "Thank you, Gideon."

She thought she saw Gideon's scowl soften for a fraction of a second, but before she could be sure, he grunted and ducked his head.

Ryan and the guys packed up the map and other documents they'd been studying.

"Everyone ready?" Ryan looked at each of them.

Shawn and Gideon nodded and grunted respectively.

Nadia swiped sweaty hands over her thighs. "Ready."

Shawn and Gideon started for the door.

Ryan stepped in front of Nadia and ran his hands up and down her forearms. "You sure you want to go along? Even if everything goes as best it could, it's bound to be emotional for you."

She went up on her toes and laid a soft kiss on his lips. "I have to do this. I'll be okay."

Ryan pulled her closer, his kiss hard and demanding. After a minute, the conspicuous throat clearing from the hall had them pulling apart, but not before they were both breathless. "This is all going to be over soon. Don't worry."

## Chapter Sixteen

It was dark when Ryan parked the rental they'd picked up at the airport behind a black Nissan Sentra. Ryan and Shawn got out of the car, leaving Gideon to watch over Nadia.

A tall African American man with wraparound aviators unfolded himself from the driver's side of the Sentra as Shawn and Ryan approached.

Shawn had given them all the lowdown on Jeremiah Griffin on the flight to Richmond. The excop turned private investigator was selective about which cases he took but owed Shawn a favor. For several hours, he'd been watching the small bungalow that Nate rented.

"A man matching your subject's description went into the house at 6:28. Looks to be watching television in the front room just off the door," Jeremiah said without preamble.

Ryan glanced at his watch. It was 8:57. Nate had been home for almost two and a half hours, long enough to settle in and relax.

"How do you want to play this?" Shawn asked.

Two pairs of eyes turned to Ryan. "We don't have a phone number for him, so we'll have to knock."

"And if he doesn't open the door?" Jeremiah said.

Ryan raised an eyebrow. "You're not a cop anymore, right?"

Jeremiah smiled wryly. "That's what they tell me."

Ryan sent Jeremiah and Shawn to cover the back while he climbed the front steps of the house. He had his gun out of its holster, but he held it down by his side so any nosy neighbors wouldn't notice it.

He knocked on the door. "Nate, it's Ryan West. Nadia sent me. Open up."

The curtain at the front window fluttered. Several moments passed with no further movement.

"I'm not very inconspicuous out here on your porch," Ryan called out. "Why don't you let me in? We can talk."

"How do I know Nadia really sent you?" Nate called from the other side of the door.

Ryan shook his head. If he'd been one of Smith's men, Nate would be dead by now, his voice giving away his location within the house.

He pulled his phone from his pocket and sent a text to Gideon. Moments later, Nadia and Gideon stepped from the car.

"Look out your window," Ryan called.

The curtain fluttered again.

"This could be a trick. You could have kidnapped her. How do I know you aren't using her to get me to open the door? Then you'll kill us both."

The vein in Ryan's neck pulsated. There was

no doubt Nate Shelton was a coward, but the man stomped on Ryan's last nerve. "If I'd wanted to kill you, you'd be dead, and I'd be on a plane back to New York already. Now, open the door."

Another minute passed before the door slowly opened.

Ryan raised his gun.

Nate peeked around the door, his eyes going wide at the sight of the gun pointed at him.

"Is anyone inside with you?" Ryan asked.

"No."

Ryan motioned to the threadbare sofa in the small living room. "Sit and don't move."

He moved down the hall, clearing the other rooms in the house and letting Shawn and Jeremiah in through the back door.

Ryan sat in the chair across from the couch while Shawn and Jeremiah took up strategic positions throughout the room. "Did Nadia really send you?" Nate asked.

"Yes. She's anxious about you," Ryan said, taking out his phone once again and texting Gideon.

Less than a minute later, the front door swung open. Nadia stepped into the house, her eyes falling on Nate the moment she entered the house.

"Nate." His name came out on a sob.

She crossed the room, sweeping her brother into a hug before he rose from the sofa. Her shoulders shook, and she held on to him as if he might disappear if she let go.

A big part of Ryan wanted to turn away from the

intimate moment between brother and sister, to give them privacy, but they didn't have the time for the Shelton siblings to work through their relationship. They needed to convince Nate that the only solution to this mess he'd gotten himself and Nadia into was for him to come back to New York and work with the authorities to take Smith down.

Ryan rose. "I'm sorry to interrupt this moment, but we have some things to talk about."

Nadia stepped out of Nate's arms and surprised them all by hauling off and punching her brother in the jaw.

Ryan stepped over the small ottoman between his chair and the sofa and grabbed Nadia's arm before she could land a second punch to Nate's face.

"How could you do this?" she hissed. "How could you be so stupid and selfish?"

Nate rubbed his jaw. "I'm sorry. I didn't mean for any of this to happen. Things just got out of control so fast."

"Let's all have a seat," Ryan said, leading Nadia to the chair he'd been sitting in.

Ryan noticed she cradled the hand she'd hit Nate with.

"I'll see if there's ice in the fridge," Jeremiah offered, noticing Nadia's injury as well.

Once Nadia and Nate sat, Ryan spoke. "We got most of the story from your uncle, but I think you owe your sister an explanation."

Nadia glared at her brother. "He owes everyone in this room an explanation. Both Ryan and I landed in the hospital because of the secrets you and Uncle Erik have been keeping."

"Uncle Erik told me about the stuff that's been happening. I didn't know things would go this far." Nate's eyes held a plea for understanding.

Ryan examined the man in front of him. Gone was the confident, fit hotel executive that appeared in the pages of background information Ryan had on Nate. This Nate was thin, his skin sallow and saggy. The last eleven months had worn on him. Ryan couldn't bring himself to feel sorry for the man.

"Well, they have. How did you get mixed up with Lincoln Smith?" Nadia said.

Nate swallowed hard. "You talked to Smith?"

Jeremiah returned with ice in a dishrag. Nadia took it from him with a nod of thanks.

"Smith ambushed Nadia in her office and demanded that she hand you over in forty-eight hours or else," Ryan said.

Nate turned to his sister with wide eyes. "And you're going to let these guys take me to him."

The anger in Nadia's eyes gave way to hurt. "Of course not."

Nate dropped his head. "It was just supposed to be a small real-estate venture. But the plan just kept growing bigger. I thought I could handle it. I wanted to prove that I wasn't just my father's son, a small-time hotelier. But I couldn't raise my half of the funds, not before the option expired. But I also didn't have ten million to pay Smith back what he'd put up for the option." Nate looked at Ryan, fear swimming in his eyes. "I know who Lincoln Smith is, and I knew he wasn't going to just write off ten million dollars."

Ryan fought the urge to knock some sense into the man. Smith might be a criminal, but he wasn't stupid. The fake-death gambit never had a chance of working. Nate was lucky he'd survived as long as he had.

"We are here to take you back to New York. Nadia is adamant that we not turn you over to Smith, even though it's what would be safest for her. And it's no more than you deserve."

Nate's head snapped up. "You don't think I know that? I know what a coward I am. I don't need you to remind me."

"We can try to get you out of this mess, but you need to come back to New York with us." Ryan paused for a second, letting his words sink in. "So what are you going to do, Nate? Are you coming with us, or are you going to leave your sister to face Smith on her own?" Ryan challenged.

It didn't matter that Nate didn't have a choice. He was going back with them one way or the other. But maybe hearing how much Nadia was willing to sacrifice for him would compel Nate to man up.

Nate stared at the floor for several long minutes.

"Nate?" Nadia said.

Nate raised his head, locking gazes with Nadia. "I'll go with you. I'll go home."

## Chapter Seventeen

The time neared two in the morning when they arrived back at the safe house in New Jersey. Nadia couldn't remember ever being more emotionally exhausted. Nate hadn't spoken to her at all on the flight, and a part of her welcomed his silence. There was so much distance and anger between them, and she wasn't sure they'd ever get back to where they used to be. The relief she felt at Nate being alive would have to be enough for now.

Until they sorted everything out, Nate would stay with Ryan and Nadia at the safe house. Given the late hour, Shawn decided to stay with them as well.

Nadia slid into bed and stared up at the ceiling. As tired as she was, sleep wouldn't come. Too much worry and…anticipation.

The soft click of her bedroom door opening finally came.

"Are you awake?" Ryan whispered.

She pushed herself up on the pillows. "Yes. I hoped you'd come."

Ryan snapped the door closed and slid into bed, drawing her to him.

"How are you doing with all this? Really?"

His hand trailed up and down her side, sending zaps of electricity running through her.

"It's almost surreal. I'd just started getting used to Nate being gone, and now he's back."

She pressed her hand to Ryan's chest and felt his heart rate pick up when she threw one of her legs on top of his and pressed in closer to his side.

"I'm glad he's alive, but…"

Ryan pressed a kiss to her forehead. "It will take some time for you and Nate to sort this all out. Don't rush yourself."

She tilted her head back so she could look into his eyes. "I don't want to talk about Nate or mobsters or either of us getting hurt right now. I just want to forget." She skimmed her hand down his bare chest to the waistband of his pajama pants. "Make me forget everything but you, Ryan."

His lips took hers softly, exploring slowly. She had been the initiator their first time together, but this time Ryan took control. His hands trailed over her body, stripping her of her nightgown before doing away with his own bottoms. He pressed his mouth to every inch of her flesh, learning what she liked, teasing and tantalizing her with every swipe of his lips or sweep of his tongue.

That they were attempting to be quiet so they didn't wake their brothers only heightened their passion.

"Ryan, please," she whispered his name, reaching for him.

He caught her hand, raising it above her head. "Unh unh unh, Miss Shelton. I'm in charge of this gorgeous body right now. I want to know every part of you tonight."

He continued to caress and tease until she was sure she couldn't take a moment more. And then he rose above her, his eyes locking on hers as he pushed himself inside her so exquisitely slowly that she was on the verge of breaking apart by the time he'd seated himself completely.

They stayed frozen that way for a moment. Then Ryan's breath hitched. Their eyes stayed locked as they moved in time with each other, slowly at first, and then faster until they reached a fever pitch.

He covered her mouth with his own as her climax hit. He followed her over the crest moments later.

They held each other afterward, whispering honeyed words of affection that led to a second round of lovemaking.

She awoke some time later, the room still too dark, even with the curtains pulled, for dawn to have broken.

She'd been too consumed with need earlier to consider whether their lovemaking might not be wise considering the injury to his side. She touched the unbandaged wound now, happy to see that it didn't appear that they'd done any more damage.

"It's fine," his sleepy voice rumbled.

"I'm just making sure. I don't need another thing to feel guilty about."

Ryan rolled, so he was on top of her. "You definitely should not feel guilty. I'd suffer through a lot more than a little cut for you."

As corny as the line was, it still brought a smile to her lips.

He kissed her, pulling away much too soon.

"Maybe I should head back to my room."

She stiffened beneath him.

"I just mean, I don't know if you want Shawn and Nate to know that I spent the night in your bed."

Nadia relaxed, a chuckle rushing through her. "It's a little late to be concerned about my virtue, don't you think?"

"Make fun if you want, but it'll be awkward walking out of this room together, half-dressed since I don't have a shirt, I might add, with our brothers out there."

She wrapped her arms tighter around him. "I don't care if your brother or my brother or anyone else knows I spent the night with you. I…care about you."

She more than cared about him. She loved him. But she suspected he'd pull away again if she told him that now. "I think we could have something real, here. If you want to try for it."

Ryan pushed a lock of hair from her forehead.

She didn't think last night was just about them letting off steam, but she wouldn't beg him to be with her either. He had to be in this as much as she was or it would never work.

He dropped his lips to hers, brushing a soft kiss over her lips. "I want to try."

That was all she needed to hear. She knew she wanted Ryan, and if they tried, they could have something incredible.

The next time she awoke, the sun peeked around the edges of the curtains, and the other side of her bed was empty. She glanced at the clock and pushed back the irritation she felt at finding Ryan gone. It was after eight in the morning, and as much as she didn't want to, they had to get up sometime.

*As soon as we settle this chaos, we'll pick a day to stay in bed all day.*

A tremor of excitement shot up her spine.

Unlike Ryan's apartment, the four bedrooms in this house shared a single bathroom.

She opened the bedroom door, and voices drifted toward her from the front of the house.

"You're the best strategist we have. We need you. Dale can cover the hotel today."

"I can coordinate with you from the hotel. We'll brief the team via video conference if we have to."

They both fell silent as Nadia stepped into the kitchen.

"Don't stop your arguing on my account," she said, grabbing a mug and pouring herself a cup of coffee.

"We're not arguing. We're just making a plan for the day," Ryan said.

Shawn frowned at his brother. "We are arguing, because your plan is stupid and won't work."

Nadia took another sip of coffee, hiding a smile. "What is—"

"My plan is not stupid." Ryan crossed his arms over his chest.

Nadia tried again. "What—"

"You are the best man we have when it comes to planning ops," Shawn said.

Irritation brewed inside her. She set her coffee mug down and turned to the sink.

Ryan and Shawn continued to argue.

Nadia gathered a bit of water in her cupped hand and flung it at the brothers.

"Hey!"

"What the—"

They broke off their staring contest to glare at her.

"Don't ignore me. Why is it a problem for Ryan to do the planning for dealing with Smith?"

"I need the team and the resources we have in our office, so I couldn't be at the hotel with you."

"I didn't come all this way to screw it all up because the best man on the team was playing baby-sitter instead of doing his job."

"Hold it, now. I didn't say he was the best man on the team," Shawn interjected.

Both she and Ryan rolled their eyes and ignored Shawn.

"If you need to be in the office, that's where you need to be." Nadia threw her hands in the air. "Smith gave us forty-eight hours. I'll be safe until they are up, but we have less than a day left."

"What is going on out here?" Nate appeared at

the kitchen entrance, his T-shirt and mesh shorts bedraggled, his feet bare.

Shawn strode across the kitchen and cupped his shoulder. "Come on in the living room. I think this conversation is headed for a place no sibling wants to witness."

Ryan growled at Shawn's back as he and Nate left the kitchen. "Jerk."

Nadia smiled. "He loves you, and you love him. Be grateful for every day you have together."

Ryan faced her, contrition painted across his handsome face. "I don't want to leave you alone."

Nadia rolled her eyes. "I'll hardly be alone at the hotel. And Dale will be there, right?"

"Yes," he muttered.

She kissed him, a smile on her lips. "I'll be fine."

"Promise?"

"Promise."

## Chapter Eighteen

Gideon arrived at the safe house to stay with Nate while Ryan escorted Nadia to work, making sure she was safely under Dale's watch before he left. Being with Ryan had been good for chasing away thoughts of mobsters, real-estate options and the millions of dollars she and Nate didn't have to pay back Smith. But now, all those worries came flooding back. What if the plan to hand Smith over to the authorities didn't work? What if it did? There would still be the problem of Nate faking his death. He'd almost certainly broken some laws. She hadn't touched the money she'd collected as the beneficiary on his insurance policy, so that wasn't an issue. Still, she wasn't sure whether there was legal liability for having accepted it. She'd have to consult a lawyer. Under normal circumstances that would be her Uncle Erik, but she wasn't ready to speak to him.

That fear and worry stayed with Nadia all morning, through her usual meetings with her managers and into the early afternoon when she would have bombed a conference call with the bank's loan officer if not for Olivia's presence.

"Why don't you go home? Take the rest of the day off?" Olivia said after Nadia had disconnected the call.

Concern stabbed Nadia. "You think it went that badly?"

"No, it's not that. You just seem so distracted. Your mind isn't here, and that's understandable."

"I'm sorry, Olivia. I've been leaving you to deal with the hotel for the last several days, and even when I'm here I'm not."

"It's fine. I can handle it."

"No, it's not fine. And yes, you are handling it well, which is why I wanted to talk to you about taking on more responsibility if you're interested."

Olivia scooted to the edge of her chair. "I'm interested."

"I've been handling most of the tasks Nate used to do with the general managers' help, but that's not a long-term answer. I need another executive, someone who can look across all the properties and help me grow the business. I thought that could be you."

"Yes!"

Nadia laughed. "You've more than proved you can handle it, even before this last week. Does the title of VP of Hotel Operations have a nice ring to it?"

Olivia squealed and bounded around the desk, catching Nadia in a hug. "Thank you. Thank you. Thank you."

"Thank you. Honestly, I wouldn't have made it

through the last eleven months without you, much less this week. You deserve the position."

Olivia returned to her seat. "You've been through a lot."

Nadia exhaled deeply. "You can say that again."

She hated keeping a secret from Olivia, but it was for the best at the moment. It wasn't clear exactly what Nate had gotten himself into, and until they knew, it was safer if no one knew he was alive. She hadn't even told Olivia about the man that attacked her and Ryan in his home, not wanting to give her friend another thing to worry about.

As if she could read Nadia's mind, Olivia asked, "Where is Ryan? He's been sticking to you like glue lately. Did something happen between you two?"

Nadia felt her cheeks heat with the memory of exactly what had happened between them.

"Oh, my goodness. Something did happen. Did the two of you—" Olivia made a gesture.

"Olivia!" Nadia thanked her lucky stars that Dale preferred to station himself outside the door to the outer office rather than sit in the office suite as Ryan did. Although, Dale's presence may have tempered Olivia's more inquisitive inclinations.

Olivia sprang out of her chair. "You did! I knew it. It's about time. You two have been circling each other like wolves for over a year. I'd begun to think it would never happen with you two."

Nadia felt her blush spread to the back of her neck. "I have not been circling anyone."

"You have. So, give me all the details." Olivia reclaimed her seat, an avid expression on her face.

"I will not. This is a place of business."

"Okay, let's go out for drinks after work tonight." Olivia held up a hand, warding off Nadia's refusal before it came. "You have to. We need to celebrate my promotion, anyway."

Nadia hesitated. "Okay, but we are celebrating your promotion. Nothing else."

"Got it. But just tell me if Ryan's a good kisser. He looks like an amazing kisser."

He'd kissed her more thoroughly than any man before him ever had, but Nadia wasn't about to confirm or deny that to Olivia. At least not without several cocktails first.

"Olivia."

"Okay, okay. I'll bug you when we're out later. But seriously, where is he? Is everything okay?"

Nadia wasn't ready to tell Olivia everything, but she wouldn't lie to Olivia either. "He's in Richmond tracking down a lead. He'll be back in the offices tomorrow."

"Oh, good. That means he's making progress. I've been so worried about you these last few days. That's part of the reason why I've wanted to do whatever I could to take some of the burden off your shoulders."

"And I'm so grateful for it." Nadia sat back. "I'm worried about Ryan. Not only did he get hurt because of this mess I'm in he also got arrested because of me."

Olivia grimaced. "Mike Dexter is such a jerk.

I can't believe he wanted you to be some fawning bubbleheaded woman when you dated. And now to manhandle you the way he did."

"Ryan and West are doing all this stuff for me—protecting me and investigating to figure out who's behind everything that's been happening. I just feel like I should do something to get Mike off of Ryan's back."

"Why don't you go talk to him? I know Mike isn't known for his compassion, but he has to have a heart in there somewhere." Olivia shrugged. "You've got nothing to lose, at least."

"I'm not as sure as you are that he has a heart, but…" An idea formed in her head.

Appealing to Mike's heartstrings would get her nowhere, but he was all about business. And she not only had something he wanted, the more she thought about it, she realized she also held his career in her hands.

"I've got an errand to run. I'll be gone for a few hours." Nadia grabbed her purse and headed for the office door.

Olivia laughed. "You're going to enjoy having a second-in-command, aren't you?"

Nadia laughed along with her. "I think I am."

Forty-five minutes later Nadia stood at the receptionist's desk at Aurora Hotels' headquarters in Tribeca, Dale standing a discreet distance behind her. Upon hearing that Nadia did not have an appointment, the brunette's smile had fallen, and she'd lost interest in feigning politeness.

"As I've explained, Mr. Dexter does not take meetings from just anyone walking off the street."

Nadia's breathing quickened, and she glared at the receptionist, fighting to keep her temper in check.

"And as I have explained, I am not just anyone off the street. My name is Nadia Shelton. I am CEO of Shelton Hotels, and Mr. Dexter and I are in the middle of a business negotiation. While I don't have an appointment, he will want to see me."

The woman's gaze slowly traveled from Nadia's head to her toes, as if she couldn't believe the woman standing in front of her was CEO of anything. The receptionist took another hard look at the business card Nadia had given her before sliding it back across the top of her desk. "Be that as it may, Mr. Dexter does not take unscheduled meetings."

Nadia didn't have the time or the patience for this little power trip.

"Tell Mr. Dexter if I'm not in his office in the next two minutes, the police will be here hauling him out in handcuffs in twenty."

The receptionist shot her a dubious look, but Nadia held the gaze. "Try me."

Apparently, it wasn't a call the receptionist was willing to make on her own. She pressed a button on her phone and then turned her back to Nadia. Her voice was a murmur, but the word *handcuffs* rang loud and clear. After several moments of silence, the receptionist swung her chair back around, replacing the handset on its cradle.

"Mr. Dexter will see you. Just around to the right and down the hall. His assistant will meet you and escort you to Mr. Dexter's office."

Dale moved to walk with her, stopping when Nadia held up a hand. "You need to stay here. I'll be fine."

Dale shook his head. "I don't know. Ryan wouldn't want me to leave you alone."

"There are dozens of people working on this floor." At his still less-than-convinced expression, she added, "If I'm not out in fifteen minutes, you have my permission to snowplow through whoever may be foolish enough to try and stop you and come find me, okay?"

He wasn't happy about it, but he took a seat in the reception area.

Nadia followed the receptionist's instructions. A lithe blonde met Nadia halfway down the hall, her pretty face marred by lips pursed as if she'd just sucked on a lemon.

"Mr. Dexter is a very busy and important man. He can only spare a few minutes."

Nadia marched toward the corner office, its large wooden door adorned with a plaque marking it as Mike's. "I won't need more than a few minutes for the business I have to take care of."

Nadia reached for the door handle, turning it and pushing into Mike's office without waiting for the assistant to announce her. The assistant bounded in behind her, apologizing for Nadia having barged in.

"It's all right, Portia. Miss Shelton and I go way back."

Portia shot one long glare at Nadia before backing from the room, closing the door as she left.

"I guess I can hardly complain, seeing as how I've made more than one unannounced trip to your office. What can I do for you, Nadia? You ready to sign on the dotted line?"

"I've been busy running a successful hotel chain, so maybe I missed the news. Has hell frozen over?"

Mike frowned. "If you aren't here for business, why are you here?"

"I'm here for business, but it has nothing to do with the hotels. I want you to drop the assault charges against Ryan West."

Mike laughed. "Now, why would I do that?"

"Because you assaulted me first. Ryan was protecting me."

"Oh, come now," Mike leaned back in his chair, his mouth drawing to one side.

"You may fancy yourself Don Draper, but it isn't 1950, and grabbing a woman and kissing her is a crime. I've already let Detective Parsmons know I'd be stopping by this afternoon."

Mike blew a raspberry. "You can't prove anything. Nobody will believe your jailbird bodyguard. But, look, I'm a reasonable man. Sell Shelton Hotels to Aurora, and I'll drop the charges. I'll even throw in the VP position for you like I offered." He flashed a cocksure grin.

Nadia placed both hands on his desk and leaned forward. "They don't have to believe him. My brand-new security system caught it all on tape. I wonder what the board will think about their president being arrested for assaulting the CEO of the company they're trying to acquire?"

Mike's grin morphed into a scowl. "I don't believe you."

Nadia smiled, stepping back from his desk. "Fine." She shrugged, pulling her cell phone from her purse and turning to leave the office. "I'll just give Detective Parsmons a call on my way out. Let him know I'm on my way to the police station."

Nadia reached for the door with one hand and lifted the phone to her ear with the other.

"Wait," Mike called out before she crossed the threshold.

Nadia held up her index finger. "One second, Mike. I'm on a call."

"Hang up the phone," he ground out between clenched teeth.

Nadia disconnected the call, not moving from the doorway. "We have a deal?"

Mike glowered, but she just waited, doing her best to remain expressionless. After a long moment, he spoke. "We have a deal."

"Great. Let's go. We have an appointment with Detective Parsmons, and I don't want to keep him waiting."

NADIA PRACTICALLY BOUNCED back into her office, with Dale trailing her.

Olivia looked up from the file she read. "Hey, you're back. I thought your errand would take longer."

"I got Mike to drop the charges against Ryan."

Olivia's eyes went wide. "You did? How?"

"I used his own dirty tactics against him. I threatened to press charges against him for grabbing me in my office the other day. No matter how much Mike's made for Aurora, the board isn't going to look the other way if I decide to press charges for his assault on me."

"So a bit of blackmail?"

Nadia narrowed her eyes at Olivia, but a smile played at her mouth.

Olivia raised her hands. "Hey, I'm here for it. I never liked Mike anyway."

"Did I miss anything?"

"No, but I'm glad you're back. There's some kind of problem in the kitchen, and a guest demanding to speak with you."

Nadia noticed Dale's eyes sharpen at Olivia's words.

"Mrs. O'Sullivan in 137. She's been a hassle since her arrival last night."

"A hassle how?" Dale asked, standing.

"The usual persnickety guest. The room we put her in last night was on too high a floor and not near an exit. The remote was missing in the room we moved her to this morning, and the temperature wouldn't set correctly. Now there's something wrong with the bathroom." Olivia rolled her eyes.

Dale relaxed.

"Why does she want to see me?" Nadia asked.

"Well, she requested to see the manager, but I can't find Stephen."

Nadia frowned. "Maybe he stepped out for a smoke."

Smoking wasn't allowed inside, obviously, and although she couldn't ban employees from smoking altogether, she'd stressed that employees who smoked should not return to work with cigarette smell lingering on their clothes. Most of the smokers hung out outside for a bit after finishing their cigarette to allow the smell to dissipate.

Nadia sighed. "I'll talk to her."

Olivia smiled. "Great. Maybe getting a private audience with the owner will get her to chill out."

"Ha. We should be so lucky." Dealing with crabby, demanding and even rude guests was just part of being in the hospitality business. Nadia had learned how to deal with them without letting them get to her long ago.

Nadia stowed her purse, and Dale followed her out of the office suite.

The hotel had a handful of rooms on the first floor, tucked away from the noise of the conference rooms and the lobby.

Room 137 was the last room in the hall and next to an emergency exit leading out into a small alleyway.

Moments after Nadia's knock, a petite woman

with gray hair pulled back into a chignon opened the door.

Nadia smiled down at the woman, extending her hand. "Mrs. O'Sullivan, I'm Nadia Shelton. I understand you haven't been having the most pleasant stay, and I wanted to see what I could do to change that."

The woman took Nadia's hand and frowned at Dale. "That's an understatement. I'd always heard good things about this hotel chain, but obviously those reviews can't be trusted," Mrs. O'Sullivan complained in a high-pitched voice.

Nadia pushed down her annoyance with the woman. "I understand we've already switched your rooms once. Is this room not more to your liking?"

"It most certainly is not. The sink is broken. How am I expected to get a good night's sleep with an incessant drip, drip, drip? Come see."

Mrs. O'Sullivan stepped away from the door and disappeared into the bathroom. Nadia hesitated for a moment, shooting a glance at Dale before stepping into the room. The bathroom was to the right of the room's door, across from the closet, its wood-slatted doors closed.

Mrs. O'Sullivan stood at the center of the bathroom, prattling on about the dripping sink. Dale followed Nadia into the room, letting the door close behind him but stopping outside the bathroom.

Nadia reached for the faucet, seeing the problem immediately. She pushed the handle backward a fraction, and the dripping ceased.

Annoyance swelled within her, but Mrs. O'Sullivan

hadn't stopped complaining long enough to allow anyone else to get a word in.

Nadia glanced over her shoulder at Dale, catching his exasperated expression before keying in on the now-open closet door and the black-clad man stepping from it.

Dale must have noticed the change in her expression. He turned, but not before the man's hand shot out. A cracking sound rang through the room as the large black stick in the man's hand made contact with the side of Dale's head.

Dale dropped to the ground, blood seeping from his wound.

Nadia stepped back as something hard was shoved in her side.

"Keep your mouth shut, and you'll be just fine." The high pitch was gone, replaced by a far more menacing tone.

The man from the closet stuck his head out into the hall. "It's clear. Let's go."

The woman dug the gun into Nadia's side. "Move."

Nadia followed the man into the hall, Mrs. O'Sullivan—or whoever the woman was—falling in step behind. Nadia glanced down the hall, hoping someone would glimpse what was going on.

As if reading her mind, the woman spoke. "I'd hurry if I was you. Having a guest shot in your hotel would probably be bad for business."

The man pushed the emergency door open. The alarm that should have sounded was mute.

A black SUV waited in the alley.

The man opened the back door. "Get in."

Nadia hesitated, calculating the likelihood of getting past her two abductors and making it to the end of the alley. The odds were not with her.

The man stepped toward her. "Get. In. Now."

Nadia turned, lifting herself into the back seat. As she did, an excruciating pain burst at the back of her head and radiated forward. Then everything went black.

## *Chapter Nineteen*

The small conference room at West was crowded when Ryan entered. He'd dispatched an operative to the safe house to babysit Nate. Now, Shawn sat at the rectangular conference table talking to Eugene. On the other side of the room, Gideon and a dark-skinned beauty with closely cropped natural hair appeared to be facing off. Gideon, his arms crossed over his large chest, stood silently stoic, as the woman, no doubt Gideon's FBI-agent friend, read him the riot act in whispered tones. Gideon's unaffected countenance seemed to increase the woman's annoyance.

Ryan raised an eyebrow, making a mental note to delve into that relationship when things settled down.

"You want to tell me what the Sam Hill you think you're doing?"

Ryan turned toward the conference door.

Detective Parsmons stood, hands on his hips, his mouth curled into a snarl.

"Why don't you have a seat, Detective, and we'll get started." Ryan waived Parsmons to the table.

Gideon and the woman with him took the hint

and headed for chairs next to Shawn. Gideon pulled out a chair for the woman, earning another eyebrow raise from Ryan.

"Get started on what?" Parsmons snarled, moving to the table and sitting heavily in a chair. Ryan took the chair next to Parsmons. "You call me and say Nathan Shelton is alive and well, and then insist I beat it down to your offices. If Shelton is alive, where is he?" Parsmons pointed across the table. "And what is the fed doing here?"

"Agent Johnson is here to help." Gideon's face showed no emotion, but his voice carried a clear warning.

Detective Parsmons narrowed his eyes at Gideon, but he wisely shut up.

Ryan made introductions around the table before getting down to the business at hand. "As you all know now, Nathan Shelton is alive." He quickly summarized how he and Nadia discovered Nate's duplicity, Erik Jackson's part in the scheme, and their trip to Richmond to pick up Nate.

"Where is Shelton now?" Parsmons asked.

"We've got him in one of our safe houses." Ryan cut Parsmons off when the detective started to object. "We've got a man with him. He's not going anywhere."

"I hate to agree with Detective Parsmons," Agent Johnson said, "but why not just hand Shelton over to the cops?"

"Because we work for Nadia Shelton," Shawn said, jumping into the conversation. "And our client is worried that her brother won't be safe in custody."

"Maybe she'll feel differently after I have her locked up for aiding and abetting fraud, harboring a fugitive and anything else I can get the district attorney to throw at her. How about that?" Parsmons said, rising.

Ryan ignored the anger bubbling in his stomach. "Sit down, Detective. Miss Shelton isn't trying to keep her brother from you. She's trying to keep him from Lincoln Smith."

Ryan explained that the reason Nathan Shelton faked his death was to get clear of a business deal he'd been involved in with the mobster that had gone south.

"We asked you here, Detective Parsmons, because we have a plan. But we'll need the NYPD to buy in. And the FBI," Ryan said.

Parsmons crossed his arms over his chest. "I can't promise anything, but let's hear it."

Ryan looked across the table at Agent Johnson. "It's well-known that the FBI has been trying to track down Smith for a while."

Agent Johnson nodded.

"Smith has given Nadia forty-eight hours to turn over Nate." Ryan looked from Agent Johnson to Detective Parsmons. "We're proposing a sting operation. We let Smith think we're turning over Nate—"

"But the feds are there for him," Parsmons interrupted. "What does the NYPD get out of this?"

"Nate Shelton," Ryan replied. "Miss Shelton understands that her brother broke the law and won't be able to just walk away from that without suffering the consequences. She simply doesn't think the consequences should include being brutally murdered by a mobster."

Parsmons seemed to consider what Ryan said. "And how do you envision this going down?"

Shawn leaned forward, steepling his hands on the table. "That's still up in the air somewhat. Actually, a lot."

"As the FBI knows well, Smith is elusive. We don't have a way to contact him, so we have to wait for him to reach out. It's doubtful he'll go for any plan we suggest."

"He definitely won't." Agent Johnson shook her head. "Smith hasn't evaded capture this long by being careless. He'll want to control all aspects of Shelton's handoff."

"We know, and we'll just have to go with that. Eugene is the best at communications. Since we have to be flexible if this has a chance of working, I wanted him in on the plans from the start. We'll need to be in constant contact with each other."

Eugene flipped the cover open on the tablet in front of him and began tapping the screen. "That's not a problem. We've got everything we need here, and I can run a centralized command center remotely if we need to."

Detective Parsmons threw up a hand. "Hang on. The NYPD hasn't agreed to anything yet."

"You have a better idea?" Ryan asked.

Parsmons glared for a long moment before turning to Agent Johnson. "Is the FBI on board with this?"

Agent Johnson shrugged. "Officially, no. I'm not here. Unofficially, we want Smith."

"In other words, the FBI is happy to take the credit, but if this whole thing goes south, you know nothing about it," Parsmons spat.

Agent Johnson touched her nose before pointing at Parsmons.

"I'll ask again. Any of you have a better idea? Because I just don't see it." Ryan looked at each of the faces around the table.

"You could just hand Shelton over to the NYPD. Let the feds worry about Smith," Parsmons offered.

"I don't think that would be in the NYPD's best interests, Detective," Agent Johnson interjected. "This is the best chance the FBI has had at getting its hands on Smith, and I think my superiors will agree that it's worth a shot. If the NYPD doesn't agree, I'm sure we can find a few federal crimes Nate Shelton's escapade violated."

Agent Johnson's implication was clear; the NYPD would get on board or be pushed out of the way.

Detective Parsmons glowered.

Ryan held up his hands to quell the interagency war threatening to break out. "Okay, I'm sure Agent Johnson and Detective Parsmons have to run this plan up their chains of command. Why don't you two do that? Gideon can show you to empty offices if you need privacy, and we'll reconvene shortly."

They all rose, and Gideon led the agent and the detective from the room. Eugene left after them to amass the equipment he thought they'd need for the operation.

Shawn circled the table, stopping beside Ryan. "What are the chances of this working?"

Ryan shook his head. "I don't know. Not great. There's too much we can't plan for. But our first priority is protecting Nadia." Ryan held his brother's gaze. "No matter what."

Shawn paused a moment, then nodded. "No matter what."

"Good. I'll call her now. I want her back at the safe house before all this goes down." Ryan punched the speed dial number for Nadia. "Who knows what Smith will do."

The phone rang four times before connecting to voice mail. He left a short message for Nadia to call him as soon as possible.

"She might be in a meeting or something. I'll try Dale," Shawn offered.

Shawn put the call on speaker, but the call once again went to voice mail.

The hair on the back of Ryan's neck rose. Nadia might be in a meeting, but Dale would have taken a call from Shawn. Unless he couldn't.

Shawn tried to call Dale a second time with the same result. He ended the call without leaving a message and dialed another number. Kevon, the operative that had taken Dale's spot manning the hotel lobby answered on the first ring.

"I need you to find out where Dale and Miss Shelton are right now," Shawn barked.

Ryan didn't hear Kevon's reply because his phone rang at that moment.

*Nadia.*

Relief flooded through him. He punched the button to accept the call.

"Nadia."

But it wasn't Nadia's voice that came from the other end of the line.

"Sorry to disappoint you." Smith's voice flowed over the line.

A moment passed before fear gave way to rage and Ryan regained the ability to speak. "Where is Nadia? If you've hurt her, I swear—"

"Calm down, Mr. West. Miss Shelton is fine. And she will remain so as long as you convey Nate Shelton to me," Smith responded.

"It hasn't been forty-eight hours."

"And yet my sources tell me you have already located Nate. I knew you were good, but I am impressed."

"Let Nadia go."

"Of course. Miss Shelton is just…a little insurance. As soon as you turn Nathan Shelton over to me, I will release her."

A knot tightened in Ryan's stomach. He knew better than to trust Smith. He should have moved faster, should never have let Nadia leave the safe house this morning.

As if he could hear his brother's thoughts, Shawn dropped a hand on Ryan's shoulder, steadying him.

"Where?" Ryan asked.

Smith gave an address.

"One hour, Mr. West. Be ready to trade."

## Chapter Twenty

Nadia opened her eyes, blinking until her glassy vision came into focus. She was lying on a cot, a flat tin roof high above her. Rolling her head to the side, she saw large windows running in a horizontal line along the midpoint of the four surrounding walls. Through their dirty panes, she could see nothing but night. She slowly pushed up to a sitting position and waited for the room to stop spinning. Her head ached, and her stomach roiled. A sound from the far side of the room drew her attention. Lincoln Smith.

"There is aspirin and water on the table next to you." Smith sat at a card table a couple dozen feet away. "My sincere apologies for my friend's heavy-handedness." Smith shot a glare at the man from the hotel room. "Rest assured we have discussed how a lady should be treated."

The same man who'd struck Dale, and presumably her, hung his head, chastised. But when Smith looked away, the man's gaze returned to Smith once more, his expression morphing into a glower that sent a chill running down Nadia's spine.

She swallowed two aspirin, washing them down with water. "Where are we?"

Smith waved away her question. "No need to worry yourself with trivial details."

"Why have you brought me here?"

"Although I like to leave innocent family members out of my business dealings, I am not a patient man. Unfortunately, you are the best motivation to get both your brother and Mr. West to do what I desire."

Icy fear raced through her veins. "Nate."

Smith shook his head. "I know this must be distressing for you."

"I have money. It will take some time, but I can come up with six million. Six million, and Nate is free of all this."

Smith looked at her with a mixture of pity and sympathy. "Making promises he could not keep is how your brother got himself into trouble. Don't make the same mistake."

Nadia glared. "That's more than half of what Nate owes you."

Smith stood and moved closer to where she still sat on the cot, forcing her to tilt her head back to maintain eye contact. "It's not about money at this point. I won't let anyone get away with humiliating me. Ripping me off. Where I come from, it would be seen as an intolerable weakness."

"So you would kill a man to allay your insecurities." Nadia didn't hide her revulsion.

Fury, dark and malicious, lit Smith's eyes. "Be careful, Miss Shelton."

The cell phone on the card table rang. Smith stepped back, snatching the phone from the table. He listened for less than ten seconds, then returned the phone to the table.

Headlights swept across the windows at the front of the warehouse.

"They're here. Get her into the office there." Smith pointed to the row of windowless offices lining the side wall of the warehouse.

The goon grabbed her arm and all but carried her to the middle office. He shoved her into the office. The door snapped shut before she'd righted herself and turned around. The lights in the room were on, probably controlled by a switch outside the door, illuminating a space with bare white walls and not much else. The office had been stripped of everything except a metal desk pushed against the wall, one of its legs propped up with a brick.

Nadia tried the handle on the door and, unsurprisingly, found it wouldn't turn. The lock looked to be nothing more than the cheap interior kind found at every hardware store in the country. It seemed of little use to break it, with Smith right outside the door, but she couldn't sit here and let Ryan and Nate walk into a trap. And she had no illusions that a trap was exactly what Smith had planned.

Voices sounded from outside the office.

"Where is Nadia?"

*Ryan!*

"Now, now, Mr. West. I promise you no harm has come to Miss Shelton. I am a man of my word."

"If you were a man of your word, Smith, Nadia wouldn't be here at all." Rage poured from Ryan's words. "Where is she?"

"Miss Shelton, would you be so kind as to let Mr. West know you are perfectly content."

*Content* wasn't exactly how she'd define her current emotional state, but Ryan sounded as if he was hanging on to his temper by a thread. The last thing the situation needed was for him to think she was hurt.

"I'm fine. I'm locked in one of the offices."

"Hang on. I'm going to get you out of here."

Not if she got out of here first. She focused on doing just that, blocking out Ryan's and Smith's angry words coming from the other side of the door. Ryan didn't want to hand Nate over to Smith before she was out of danger. Smith was not in agreement with that plan.

Nadia looked up. If the office door wasn't an option…

White pockmarked drop panels formed the ceiling. She doubted the panels would hold her weight, but maybe she could crawl along the top of the wall.

*And go where?*

Dropping into the middle of the warehouse floor onto a group of men who undoubtedly carried more weapons than she'd ever laid eyes on did not seem a good idea. Yet, staying in this room left her a sitting duck. Even if she was only able to shift over an office or two she'd have the element of surprise on her side.

She hauled herself onto the desk and teetered for a moment before finding her balance like a surfer catching a wave. Once she was sure the desk wouldn't throw her off, she pushed the panel closest to her up and away from the metal frame.

Taking a deep breath, she jumped, grabbed the top of the wall and pulled herself onto its narrow width.

She exhaled exhilaration and fear and began crawling along the wall.

"This is getting tiresome," Smith's agitated voice carried into the ceiling. "Produce Mr. Shelton, or I'll have my man here put a bullet in your pretty little girlfriend. I'm sure you don't think you can dispatch me and get to her before a bullet does."

She didn't wait for Ryan's response.

The ceiling of the office next to the one she'd been in was missing several tiles. It wasn't as far as she'd hoped to get, but from what she'd heard, she didn't have long before someone came looking for her.

She crawled to the adjacent office. Thankfully, the setup here was the same as in the office she'd left, with the desk pushed against the wall. Unlike the office she'd come from, this one did have a small window near the door.

She dropped down onto the desk, careful to stay out of view. She froze at the thud of her feet meeting the desktop. Seconds passed, and no one rushed through the door.

A pile of crumpled clothes near the desk caught her eye. It took a moment for her to realize that someone wore the clothes.

It looked like Smith had caught up with his rogue employee. Taras Ledebev lay on the floor, his face a bloody patchwork of bruises. His chest fell in slow, shallow breaths that made it clear he was in serious trouble.

The whine of a metal door opening filled the warehouse.

"Mr. Shelton. I'm glad you could finally join us."

She chanced a peek through the window.

Ryan stood beside Nate, steps inside the warehouse's open door, his gun held outstretched toward Smith. Smith had adopted a similar posture with his stance and gun.

She wouldn't let Nate turn himself over to a killer to save her.

"I'm here. Now let my sister go."

Nadia heard the door in the next room open.

A beat past. "She's gone."

Anger hardened Ryan's face. "What game are you playing, Smith?"

"She must be in one of those rooms. Find her," Smith barked.

Nadia scanned the room for something to defend herself with. This office had been stripped similar to the other, but a broom and bucket had been left in a corner. It wasn't much of a plan, but if she could incapacitate Smith's helper, it would increase the odds in their favor.

She grasped the broom in a batter's stance and waited to the side of the door.

The door swung open, and Smith's goon stomped in, gun in hand.

Nadia swung the broom handle, connecting with

the man's hard stomach with enough force to send vibrations up her arm.

He bent at the waist, his large frame blocking the door. He'd had the wind knocked out of him, but he was rallying fast.

She raised the broom again, preparing to bring it down across the back of his neck.

The man raised his gun. "I wouldn't do that if I was you. Drop it."

Nadia opened her hands and let the broom fall to the floor.

"Move." The man waved his gun toward the door, stepping away from it to give her room to exit.

She took pride in the fact that he was still hunched a bit as he followed her out of the office.

Smith smiled without looking at her. "You are a fighter, I'll give you that, Miss Shelton. But I tire of these games." His smile dropped. "An even exchange, Mr. West? Miss Shelton will walk toward you at the same time Mr. Shelton makes his way to me, yes?"

"No!" Nadia called out.

"Shut up." The man behind her pushed her forward, farther from the office.

Ryan's eyes narrowed, never leaving Smith's face. He nodded assent.

"Okay. Move." Smith waved her toward Ryan and Nate with his gun. "But not too fast."

Nadia took a step, and Nate did the same.

Another step forward. Nate stepped forward too. She felt as if she was involved in a weird mirror-image wedding march, but this was no happy occasion. Nate was effectively walking to his death. She couldn't let that happen.

Nadia stopped walking halfway between Smith and Ryan.

"I'm sorry I got you mixed up in this. I'm sorry for everything," Nate said, his eyes glassy with unshed tears.

"Nate, don't do this. You can't trade yourself for me." Nadia didn't try to stop her tears from falling.

"Don't worry, sis. Everything will be all right. Just keep walking." Nate stepped away from her, toward Smith.

She turned, a hand outstretched to reach for Nate.

"Nadia, come on. Let me get you out of here, sweetheart."

Ryan still held his gun pointed at Smith, but his gaze flicked to hers for a moment. She wasn't sure whether he was trying to communicate something to her or if it was just unbridled hope that this was part of a plan to get them all out of this unscathed, but she dropped her hand and moved forward.

It felt like hours, but she finally made it to Ryan's side.

"Keep going, sweetheart. I'll be right behind you."

"No. Not without Nate." The words barely escaped her mouth before a pair of large arms thrust through the open warehouse doors, grabbing her and yanking her into the dark night.

Behind her, glass shattered, and men shouted incomprehensible words. Three thunderous booms preceded a flash and the rapidly repeated bangs that could only be gunfire.

Nadia felt herself being lifted, and then the world turned upside down. Her torso made contact with a broad shoulder, knocking the wind from her for a moment. The ground sped by beneath her.

Moments later, she was placed on her feet and looked up into Shawn West's eyes.

The fear-fueled temper she'd been ready to unleash died at the sight of the warehouse.

Smoke billowed out of the shattered windows, and flames licked the roof. The blue door Shawn pulled her through was gone, a gaping hole where it had been.

"Ryan!"

A beefy arm wrapped around her waist, keeping her from running back toward the warehouse.

"No. You need to get checked out by the medics," Shawn said, showing no signs of strain against her struggling.

"But Nate and Ryan are still in there!"

"Ryan is good at what he does. If anyone can get himself and your brother out of there, it's him. And the first thing both of them will want to know is that you are okay."

Nadia let Shawn lead her to the back of an ambulance. He was right. There was nothing she could do but get out of the way.

There were people everywhere, many wearing windbreakers embossed with *FBI*, others clad in black and wearing bulletproof vests.

*Please let Ryan and Nate have on bulletproof vests.*

She knew what gunfire sounded like, and there had been more than enough bullets fired to take down both men.

She stared at the warehouse, trying to identify Ryan and Nate among the people moving in and around the building. The frantic pace of her rescuers slowed, and three fire trucks moved in to begin dealing with the flames.

Still, there was no sign of Ryan or Nate.

"Nadia." Nate's weary voice sounded seconds before he rounded the open ambulance doors, leaning heavily on Ryan.

She wasn't sure which man to hug first, so she threw her arms around them both, dragging them into a three-person hug.

Nate groaned, and Nadia pulled back, the relief that had soared through her at seeing Nate and Ryan in one piece replaced by concern.

"Nate took two in the chest. He had a vest on," Ryan added quickly, "but he'll still need to go get checked out, and he'll be sore for a while."

Ryan helped Nate lower himself into the back of the ambulance, then stepped away so the EMTs would have room.

Nadia stepped into Ryan's arms, carefully this time in case he too had been injured. She tilted her head back so she could look into his eyes. "Thank you."

"Mr. Shelton, I'm Agent Kenzi Johnson with the Federal Bureau of Investigation. I'll be accompanying you to the hospital."

Nadia tensed, and Ryan ran a hand up and down her back. It was too much to hope that Nate would get out of the mess he'd made completely unscathed. She didn't know what the penalty was for faking one's death, but whatever it was, they'd deal with it. Nate and Ryan were alive, and that was what she wanted to concentrate on now.

A throat cleared behind them. "I'll pick you up at the hospital," Gideon said, the statement obviously meant for Agent Johnson.

The agent narrowed her eyes at Gideon. "That won't be necessary."

"I'll stop by the coffee shop you like on the way," Gideon continued as if Agent Johnson hadn't spoken. "Mocha caramel latte, right?"

A low growl sounded in Agent Johnson's throat. "Fine. Do what you like. I don't have time to argue with you. I have to interview a witness."

Agent Johnson hoisted herself into the back of the ambulance with Ryan.

Ryan's, Shawn's and even Nadia's mouths fell open at the sight of Gideon's mouth curling into a smile.

The ambulance doors closed, and moments later it raced away from the scene.

"I can't believe it," Shawn said, his voice full of awe as he watched Gideon stroll away, a definite skip in his step. "You and Gideon have women, and I'm single. How is that even possible?"

Ryan dropped a hand on his brother's shoulder and pulled Nadia closer to his side. "You know what they say, bro. Love comes at you when you least expect it."

## Chapter Twenty-One

Ryan had shot Smith and the man who'd kidnapped Nadia. Smith's wound would heal, but the other man hadn't been as lucky. Neither was Taras. Both men had succumbed to their wounds on the way to the hospital. Nadia wasn't sure how she felt about the men's deaths. On the one hand, they were the criminals who'd kidnapped her. On the other hand, they'd been killed so she could be saved. It was something she'd have to deal with in the coming days.

One thing she wouldn't have to worry about was Smith. He was somewhere in the hospital in FBI custody, under whose mandate he'd likely stay for the rest of his natural life, based on the information Agent Johnson had shared.

"The FBI aren't the only ones with good news," Detective Parsmons stated once Agent Johnson finished. "We caught a man attempting to set fire to a business in Lower Manhattan. An arsonist for hire. He was quick to give up his many contractors, one of whom was Mike Dexter."

Parsmons's words hit Nadia with a force similar to a knock to the head. "What! Why?"

Parsmons rocked back on his heels, happy to be the center of attention. "Mr. Dexter lawyered up, but his arsonist kept detailed notes and recordings for just such an occasion. It was all part of Mr. Dexter's campaign to get you to sell Shelton Hotels."

Even with all that she'd just been through, it was hard to believe Mike would go so far in his quest to get Shelton. And she planned to do everything she could to make sure he didn't weasel out of the consequences.

Parsmons and Agent Johnson said their goodbyes and headed for the exit. Nadia watched as the federal agent left the hospital through the ER entrance and strolled toward the black SUV Gideon leaned against. Gideon opened the passenger door for the agent. She paused at the open door, saying something that made Gideon throw back his head in laughter before getting in.

Nadia glanced at Ryan, whose mouth hung open like the clown at a carnival ball-toss game, just waiting for someone to toss a ball in.

It was a nice, if short, break from wondering whether Nate was okay.

She'd insisted Ryan drive her straight to the ER, but the doctors hadn't allowed her to see Nate. Ryan assured her Nate would be okay, that the bulletproof vest had caught the worst of it, but she wouldn't stop worrying until she saw for herself that Nate was fine.

As worried as she was about Nate, she couldn't help replaying in her mind something Ryan had said.

*Love comes at you when you least expect it.*

Love. Did he mean that he loved her? Because she knew without a doubt that she loved him. Had loved him since the day, over a year ago, when he'd first walked into her office. Whether it was propriety, professionalism or just simple fear that had been keeping her from admitting it, it wouldn't stop her from going after what she wanted now. And what she wanted was Ryan West in her life. Forever.

She glanced at him, and he squeezed her hand. "Nate's tough. He'll be okay."

The doors marked *Authorized Personnel* slid open, and a doctor strolled into the waiting room. "Miss Shelton?"

"That's me." She hurried toward the doctor, Ryan on her heels.

"Your brother will be fine. He's bruised, but none of the bullets penetrated his skin. We're going to keep him here for observation overnight, just as a precaution. He inhaled quite a bit of smoke, and we want to make sure there's no damage to his lungs."

She exhaled heavily. "Thank goodness."

"The police said it would be okay for you to go in and see him, if you'd like," the doctor said.

Her relief flagged at the reminder that even when Nate left the hospital, it might not be for home. Nadia and Ryan passed through the doors the doctor had come through, still holding hands. It wasn't difficult to discern which cubicle Nate was in. A uniformed

NYPD officer stood at attention in front of only one of the curtained areas that lined either side of the ER.

The officer nodded at them, obviously having been told that they were okay to enter.

Ryan stopped outside the curtain. "I'll wait for you here."

She bussed a kiss on his cheek. She was ready to share her life with Ryan, but her relationship with Nate was in a precarious place. She preferred that these opening salvos into whatever relationship they might have going forward be made in private.

Nate's eyes were closed when Nadia pushed through the curtain.

His face was gray, and the strain of the last year showed in the lines that marred his face.

"Nate."

His eyes opened, and his lips turned up into a trembling smile. "I wasn't sure you'd want to see me ever again."

Nadia reached for her brother's hand, surprised to feel hot tears on her cheeks. "I just spent eleven months thinking you were dead. Of course I want to see you."

"I'm so sorry, Nadia." Nate's voice broke. "I just didn't know what else to do."

"We've got a lot to talk about. But you, me and Uncle Erik, we're all the family each other has, and we'll work through it."

She stayed with Nate a few more minutes before promising to be in touch the next day.

Ryan waited on the other side of the curtain. "You ready?"

She nodded, falling in step next to him.

They were silent on the walk from the hospital to the car.

Ryan held the passenger door to his SUV open for her just as Gideon had for Agent Johnson, and just like the agent, Nadia paused before getting in the car.

"You can drop me off at my apartment."

Ryan's mouth turned down in a frown. "Is that what you want?"

Her gaze swept the ground. "I can't keep imposing on you. Smith isn't a threat anymore."

"No, he isn't. And he's not why I want you to stay with me tonight either."

Nadia looked into Ryan's eyes. "You want me to stay."

"I do. I know I said I wanted to keep things professional between us, but I lied. It's never just been a working relationship with us, least of all these last few days."

Nadia felt heat rise on the back of her neck at the thought of just how unprofessional they'd acted several times over the last few days. Still, she wouldn't have changed a thing.

She smiled. "No, it hasn't been. I want to see where this goes. I haven't exactly had great luck in the relationship department, but I think you just might be the man to change that, Ryan West."

She moved around the open door and slid her arms around his waist.

His arms came around her, drawing her close. "You know, I have been told I am the best at what I do."

His mouth met hers, proving that he was, in fact, the best at one thing.

\* \* \* \* \*

"I don't know anything," she said. "Why does TDC think
I do?"

"I don't know." Was this an especially bold gambit on
TDC's part, or merely a desperate one?

"Maybe this isn't about what TDC wants you to reveal,"
he said. "Maybe it's about what they think you know that
they don't want you to say."

She pushed her hair back from her forehead, a distracted
gesture. "I don't understand what you're getting at."

"Everything TDC is doing—the charges against your
father, the big reward, the publicity—those are the actions
of an organization that is desperate to find your father."

"Because they want to stop him from talking?"

"I could be wrong, but I think so."

Most of the color had left her face, but she remained
strong. "That sounds dangerous," she said. "A lot more
dangerous than diapers."

"You don't have any idea what TDC might be worried about?" he asked. "It could even be something your father mentioned to you in passing."

"He didn't talk to me about his work. He knew I wasn't interested."

"What did you talk about?" Maybe the answer lay there.

"What I was doing. What was going on in my life." She shrugged. "Sometimes we talked about music, or movies, or books. Travel—that was something we both enjoyed. There was nothing secret or mysterious or having anything to do with TDC."

"If you think of anything else, call me." It was what he always said to people involved in cases, but he hoped she really would call him.

"I will." Did he detect annoyance in her voice?

"What will you do about the lawsuit?" he asked.

She looked down at the white envelope. "I'll contact my attorney. The whole thing is ridiculous. And annoying." She shifted her gaze to him at the last word. Maybe a signal for him to go.

"I'll let you know if I hear any news," he said, moving toward the door.

"Thanks."

"Try not to worry," he said. Then he added, "I'll protect you." Because it was the right thing to say. Because it was his job.

Because he realized nothing was more important to him at this moment.

*Don't miss*
Mountain Investigation *by Cindi Myers,*
*available March 2021 wherever*
*Harlequin Intrigue books and ebooks are sold.*

Harlequin.com

HIEXP0221

# Get 4 FREE REWARDS!

## We'll send you 2 FREE Books plus 2 FREE Mystery Gifts.

**WHAT SHE DID**
BARB HAN

**HOSTILE PURSUIT**
JUNO RUSHDAN

**Harlequin Intrigue** books are action-packed stories that will keep you on the edge of your seat. Solve the crime and deliver justice at all costs.

**FREE** Value Over **$20**

---

**YES!** Please send me 2 FREE Harlequin Intrigue novels and my 2 FREE gifts (gifts are worth about $10 retail). After receiving them, if I don't wish to receive any more books, I can return the shipping statement marked "cancel." If I don't cancel, I will receive 6 brand-new novels every month and be billed just $4.99 each for the regular-print edition or $5.99 each for the larger-print edition in the U.S., or $5.74 each for the regular-print edition or $6.49 each for the larger-print edition in Canada. That's a savings of at least 12% off the cover price! It's quite a bargain! Shipping and handling is just 50¢ per book in the U.S. and $1.25 per book in Canada.* I understand that accepting the 2 free books and gifts places me under no obligation to buy anything. I can always return a shipment and cancel at any time. The free books and gifts are mine to keep no matter what I decide.

Choose one:  ☐ **Harlequin Intrigue Regular-Print** (182/382 HDN GNXC)     ☐ **Harlequin Intrigue Larger-Print** (199/399 HDN GNXC)

Name (please print)

Address                                                                 Apt. #

City                            State/Province                    Zip/Postal Code

**Email:** Please check this box ☐ if you would like to receive newsletters and promotional emails from Harlequin Enterprises ULC and its affiliates. You can unsubscribe anytime.

### Mail to the **Reader Service:**
**IN U.S.A.:** P.O. Box 1341, Buffalo, NY 14240-8531
**IN CANADA:** P.O. Box 603, Fort Erie, Ontario L2A 5X3

Want to try 2 free books from another series? Call 1-800-873-8635 or visit www.ReaderService.com.

*Terms and prices subject to change without notice. Prices do not include sales taxes, which will be charged (if applicable) based on your state or country of residence. Canadian residents will be charged applicable taxes. Offer not valid in Quebec. This offer is limited to one order per household. Books received may not be as shown. Not valid for current subscribers to Harlequin Intrigue books. All orders subject to approval. Credit or debit balances in a customer's account(s) may be offset by any other outstanding balance owed by or to the customer. Please allow 4 to 6 weeks for delivery. Offer available while quantities last.

Your Privacy—Your information is being collected by Harlequin Enterprises ULC, operating as Reader Service. For a complete summary of the information we collect, how we use this information and to whom it is disclosed, please visit our privacy notice located at corporate.harlequin.com/privacy-notice. From time to time we may also exchange your personal information with reputable third parties. If you wish to opt out of this sharing of your personal information, please visit readerservice.com/consumerschoice or call 1-800-873-8635. Notice to California Residents—Under California law, you have specific rights to control and access your data. For more information on these rights and how to exercise them, visit corporate.harlequin.com/california-privacy.

HI20R2

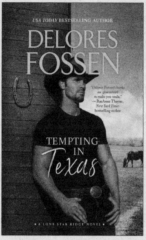